Y0-BVF-502

An Autographed Mystery

DeAnna Julie Dodson

AnniesFiction.com

Books in the Secrets of the Castleton Manor Library series

A Novel Murder
Bitter Words
The Grim Reader
A Deadly Chapter
An Autographed Mystery
Second Edition Death
A Crime Well Versed
A Murder Unscripted
Pride and Publishing
A Literary Offense
Up to Noir Good
For Letter or Worse
On Pens and Needles
Ink or Swim
Tell No Tales
Page Fright
A Fatal Yarn
Read Between the Crimes
From Fable to Grave
A Fateful Sentence
Cloak and Grammar
A Lost Clause
A Thorny Plot
A Scary Tale Wedding

Library of Congress-in-Publication Data
An Autographed Mystery/ by DeAnna Julie Dodson
p. cm.
I. Title
2017945424

AnniesFiction.com
(800) 282-6643
Secrets of the Castleton Manor Library™
Series Creator: Shari Lohner
Series Editors: Jane Haertel and Janice Tate
Cover Illustrator: Jesse Reisch

10 11 12 13 14 | Printed in South Korea | 9 8 7 6 5 4 3

1

Faith Newberry pulled her cable-knit wool sweater more tightly around her shoulders, certain the temperature was dropping even inside the library of Castleton Manor. It had been a cold February so far, and, judging by the baleful gray of the sky, that seemed unlikely to change in the next day or two. Still, she felt cozy enough seated before the roaring fire and surrounded by two levels of floor-to-ceiling bookcases, though she didn't know if she would ever get used to the sheer opulence of the room or of the rest of the manor.

A blast of wind rattled the windows, and Faith got up to peer outside. This would be the worst time for a storm. Not that the manor wasn't lovely with a fluffy white layer of snow on the roof and covering the grounds, but she had worked too hard to get everything arranged for the Drelincourt family reunion to see it summarily canceled due to bad weather.

"Don't snow," she whispered to the darkening sky. "Don't snow, don't snow, don't snow, don't—"

"What did you say?"

Faith jumped and then turned around to see a waifish blonde girl in the black pants and white blouse the housekeeping staff typically wore. "Laura, don't do that."

The young woman turned fiery red. "I'm so sorry. I didn't mean to—I wasn't—"

Faith chuckled. "It's all right. You just startled me. I was hoping the weather wouldn't spoil things for us."

"I guess there's always a good chance of that." Laura stared out the window. "Is something special going on?"

Faith nodded and moved away from the chilly window to warm herself again at the fire. "I'm hoping to make a nice acquisition for the manor library, if the sellers can get here without any problems."

"Oh, that's exciting." Laura's normally mild expression was suddenly eager as she gazed around the room. "It's such an amazing collection already. I bet those new books will be a wonderful addition."

"*If* I can get the owners to sell," Faith told her. "Sometimes these negotiations can be a little bit tricky."

Laura laughed shyly. "I bet you can do it. And then maybe Ms.—"

"Laura!"

Laura spun around, somehow managing to knock an antique globe and a stack of slick magazines off the desk. "Ms. Russell." She scrambled to put everything back in place, toppling the telephone off its charger and upsetting a coffee cup full of pens and pencils as she did.

Marlene Russell, assistant manager of Castleton Manor, glared down her pointed nose, a picture of perfectly groomed disdain. "I thought you were preparing the Drelincourt rooms."

"I am. I mean, I was. I did." Laura put the pens and pencils back into the cup and promptly spilled them again.

"She came to tell me the rooms were ready and to ask if there was anything she could do to help me before our guests arrive," Faith said smoothly, earning an expression of profound gratitude from the younger woman. "You haven't heard anything from them, have you? They're still coming?"

"Not a word," Marlene replied. "Things seem to be on schedule. I just hope bad weather doesn't hit before they all get here safely." She turned her attention back to Laura, making her almost spill the pens and pencils for a third time. "So you've got that entire block of rooms spotless and ready to go?"

Laura nodded and put the pencil cup on the desk.

Marlene frowned. "Go and see if there's anything you can assist with in the kitchen."

"Yes ma'am. Thank you." Laura glanced at Faith, then scrambled out of the library.

"She only wants to help," Faith said after a moment.

Marlene crossed her arms. "If she wants to help, she could start by doing the job she gets paid for."

"It sounds like she did that already." Faith softened her voice. "Listen, it's a slow day, and Laura loves the library. What would it hurt for her to help out in here sometimes?"

Marlene raised one eyebrow and looked pointedly at the disarrayed desk.

"She was fine," Faith said, putting things straight again, "until you came in and scared her out of her wits."

The assistant manager's disdain turned into disgust. "I did no such thing. I don't know why you would say something like that. I didn't scare her."

"She really wants to improve herself," Faith said, passing over that last remark. "I don't blame her for wanting to do something more interesting than cleaning up after our guests and their pets. And to tell the truth, I could use a little assistance once in a while."

Now Marlene raised both eyebrows. "Are you telling me you can't handle your job?"

Faith resisted the urge to roll her eyes. "No, of course not. But I wish you'd at least let Laura give it a try. Like an intern."

Marlene huffed. "I don't know why you're so interested in her anyway. I'd think you'd be much more concerned about charming the Drelincourts into selling us their Agatha Christie collection." She sat in the leather chair across from Faith and crossed her ankles. "What have you found out about them so far?"

"Not much," Faith admitted. "There are ten of them, all grandchildren of Jamison Drelincourt, the investor. He divided up the books his father had collected as evenly as possible among the grandchildren. Together, it's quite a valuable lot."

"Are you sure you're up to something like this? I can't imagine you negotiated sales of this magnitude when you were working at Hawarden."

Faith refused to take offense at the obvious dig at her competence and experience. "Not at a university that size, no, but I've done my research. I know what each first edition is worth, autographed and in mint condition, and that we'll have to pay more than that for a complete collection. Then we'll need to add a premium because each volume was purchased by just one man, Jamison's father, Archibald, at the time of first publication. Since the books came out between 1920 and 1976, that's quite an amazing feat."

Marlene managed a sour smile. "What's amazing is that Archie's great-grandchildren didn't sell them off the minute they inherited them."

"Their grandfather, Jamison, inherited them first, and I think he anticipated that might be how it would be with the grandchildren, so they're really held in trust by their uncle. He'd have to give his consent as far as selling them or anything like that is concerned anyway."

"That's the Maxwell Drelincourt who's hosting the reunion."

Faith nodded. "I suppose you talked to him when he made the arrangements. What's he like?"

"I did talk to him," Marlene said, "but only briefly. He had his niece Tilly handle the details for him. Still, he seemed pleasant enough. An old-fashioned gentleman. I gave him the Agatha Christie Suite, since it seemed particularly fitting, and put Tilly in the Jane Austen Suite. The other nine cousins are on either side of them, filling up that part of the floor. We don't have anyone else booked until the Western romance writers come a week from Wednesday, so we'll be able to give the eleven of them our undivided attention."

"Only eleven? No spouses? Children? Significant others?"

Marlene shook her head. "Tilly said that her uncle wanted to spend time with just his nieces and nephews. I got the impression that the family had drifted apart since the grandfather's passing."

"That's too bad. I'm fortunate enough to have a tight-knit family, but so many people don't." Faith gathered up the papers scattered on the desk, mostly information about comparable sales of Christie books and other noted collections. "Good for him, trying to keep them close. We'll have to make their stay memorable."

"I'm sure the most memorable thing for them would be getting a good price for their books. Have you discussed all this with Wolfe?" Marlene glanced up to the frescoed ceiling above them. The third floor of Castleton Manor was owner Wolfe Jaxon's private residence, not open to guests.

Faith involuntarily followed her gaze. "Certainly. We've agreed on what would be a reasonable price for the collection, so I know what my limits are. Fortunately, the Drelincourts don't know that."

Marlene pursed her lips. "It seems to me that something like this ought to be handled by Wolfe himself. That's a lot of money you'll be playing with."

"I won't be playing," Faith said, and then she made her expression more pleasant. Marlene Russell was not going to get her rattled. Not today. "You keep the family well fed and comfortable, and I'll see to the negotiations. That's not to say that Wolfe won't be involved, of course. The final yea or nay will be his, but I'll be the one seeing to the details."

Faith had gaped at Wolfe when he told her he wanted her to take charge of the acquisition, but he'd been on his way to a meeting at the time, so she hadn't had the opportunity to really discuss it with him. "I trust you to take care of it for me," he'd said, and then he'd hurried out to his BMW.

She replayed the words in her head now. *I trust you to take care of it for me.* She would do her job, and she'd do it extremely well. And she'd have an ally.

She smiled, more to herself than Marlene. "So what do you think about Laura? Can we give her a try here in the library for a few hours a week?"

"Right now?" There was an expression of near horror on Marlene's face. "With the Drelincourts coming and a major acquisition in the works? And you want to start her now?"

"She'll do fine. I promise you, you'll never find anyone who tries harder."

"Trying hard won't get the books shelved properly."

"Then I'll make sure she learns how to do it right," Faith said. "There's not that much to it."

"There's not much to serving soup, but she still managed to get some on Wolfe's mother the last time she was here."

Faith winced. "That's not good. But Laura's less nervous around me than she would be around Charlotte."

"She'll probably spill coffee on the Drelincourt copy of *The Mysterious Affair at Styles*," Marlene grumbled. "Right over the autograph."

Faith laughed softly. She could tell Marlene was weakening. "Just give her a chance. You know how important it is for this to go well. It would be an incredible acquisition for the library. I'm not going to let anything spoil it. Laura will be fine. I'll stay with her every moment she's in here, especially when the

Drelincourts are around, and we won't drink any coffee. What do you say?"

Marlene pressed her lips together, eyeing Faith as if she didn't know whether to scold her or simply wash her hands of the whole thing. "Well, if it were up to me, I wouldn't let Laura get closer to the library than running a vacuum cleaner over the carpet."

"She's not that bad." Faith gave her an innocent smile. "Or should I ask Wolfe what he thinks?"

"No, don't bother him with this," Marlene groused. "Besides, you know what he'd say."

"Of course I do," Faith said, certain that Wolfe would help someone like Laura if he could. "That's why I offered to ask him about it."

"Fine. If you want to try her out, go ahead. Temporarily. And only in addition to her regular duties. I don't have anybody available to do her job for her. But don't come crying to me if she spoils things with the Drelincourts."

Faith had yet to go crying to Marlene about anything since she'd been at the manor, so she didn't know why she would suddenly start. But she made no mention of that just now. "Thank you," she said instead. "And I think the timing is good. At least we don't have one of our retreats going on. With only eleven guests, I should have plenty of time to show her the ropes."

"And with her around," Marlene said, "plenty of knots to untangle."

2

Faith found Laura in the butler's pantry scrubbing the already-immaculate floor. "I'm afraid I have bad news for you."

Laura stared up at her, her face pale. "I'm fired, right? Ms. Russell's finally had enough of my clumsiness." She pushed herself up and sat back on her heels. "I knew I should have kept my head down and not said anything to anyone. I'm sorry I got you involved." She blew a strand of hair out of her eyes, the picture of forlorn resignation.

"No, no, that's not it." Faith grinned and helped her to her feet. "It's just that you're going to have less free time from now on."

"What do you mean?"

"She said it was okay if you start helping me in the library."

Laura blinked at her, and then a bewildered smile crept across her face. "You mean—really?"

"Really. Now, it will be temporary. Only in your free time, and you can't get behind on your other work. We'll try it out for a little while, and if you like it, then you're going to have to get serious about going back for your degree in library science."

"Ms. Russell's not mad?"

"No." Faith chuckled. "Well, not any more than usual anyway."

Laura shrugged. "I guess she's got a lot on her mind. Ms. Newberry, I don't mean to—"

"Stop right there. First off, if we're going to be working together, you'd better start calling me Faith like everybody else does. I don't want to think you're talking to my mother or anything."

"All right . . . Faith." Laura ducked her head. "Anyway, I don't mean to be such a klutz, but Ms. Russell makes me so nervous that I just can't help it. I'm always worse when she's around."

"I know she can be intimidating. Trust me, I feel like I'm all thumbs and left feet sometimes when I'm talking to her. But I'm pretty sure she's not going to bite either of us. At least I hope not."

Laura nodded, not appearing quite convinced.

"Seriously," Faith said, "she's no different from anyone else. I know she's had some tough times in the past. I expect being a little prickly is her way of protecting herself from getting hurt again."

"I suppose."

Faith gave her a warm smile. "If you don't know what to do, ask me. Remember that I'm on your side. That doesn't sound too hard, does it?"

"That doesn't sound hard at all. It sounds nice."

"Now when you're finished here, you come find me and we'll talk about what we need to do when the Drelincourts get in. I'm going to see if Mr. Jaxon has time to talk to me for a minute, but then I'll be in the library."

"Okay. I'm nearly done, so I'll get cleaned up and then meet you there."

"That would be perfect." Faith glanced at her watch. "I'll see you in the library."

With a little wave, Faith left the butler's pantry and headed back toward the library. She stopped for a moment in the Great Hall gallery to admire the statue of Agatha Christie, poised to write her latest mystifying plot.

"If we're going to make you stand there day in and day out, it only seems right that we should have a complete set of your first editions in our library, doesn't it? I hope I can pull this off."

"Of course you can."

Faith caught a breath and turned around. Wolfe Jaxon was smiling at her, flawless as always in a designer suit and tie and—she was sure—handmade Italian shoes.

"You really shouldn't sneak up on people," she said, smiling back. "Not when they're having conversations with the queen of the murder mystery."

He spread one hand over his crisp white shirtfront. "I promise I haven't killed anyone all day. I'm glad I caught you, though. I wanted to make sure everything's ready for when the Drelincourts arrive. I'll try my best to return before then, but I might not make it, especially with the weather like it is."

"I'm sure they'll understand if you're delayed, but I'd feel better if you were here." Faith bit her lip, wondering if she should say anything else, but she couldn't help herself. As Marlene had reminded her, this was an important acquisition. She didn't want to let anyone down, especially Wolfe. "Are you sure you shouldn't have one of your attorneys handling this? Or one of your financial people? I mean, yes, I handled this kind of thing at Hawarden but never involving this much money."

"Don't worry about any of that. You've done your homework on the collection. The lawyers and finance guys can check it all over once you make the deal."

"But I thought you'd be in on at least some of this."

His blue eyes crinkled at the corners as he smiled. "My dad always told me to hire good people and then let them do their jobs. You're good people, Faith. I trust you to do your job." He checked his watch. "I'm sorry. I'd love to stay and talk, but I'm running late. Knock 'em dead, okay?" In a few long strides, he had crossed the gallery and was gone.

Faith exhaled. No wonder his employees loved him. How could they not?

"Faith!"

Faith turned at the familiar voice and saw Brooke Milner, the manor's sous-chef, coming from the breakfast room, her blue eyes lit with excitement.

"Nice job," she said, displaying her usual perky grin. "You know, I waited for a minute before I said anything. Just in case Wolfe didn't want to be interrupted."

Faith laughed and shook her head. "We were talking about the Drelincourt collection. All business."

There was a sudden twinkle in Brooke's eye, the same one she got when the Candle House Book Club was discussing a scene from a book with a little sizzle in it. "It seemed pretty chummy from where I was standing."

"Then I think you must have been standing in the wrong place."

"All right, all right," Brooke said, holding up both hands in surrender. "But just you wait."

"I won't hold my breath."

"Whatever you say. Anyway, I came to ask you about tonight's dinner. The head chef's out of town, and I know you want it to be perfect. I was planning to serve crostini with white truffle oil and lavender, but I'm out of olive paste, and with this bad weather, I hate to go out for some and get stuck somewhere. Do you think we'll be fine without the crostini?"

Faith smiled. Brooke always wanted Castleton Manor meals to be not only delicious but productions in and of themselves. "I've seen tonight's menu. I think the Drelincourts will be so impressed with everything else that they'll never even think of crostini."

"Good. Well, I'd better get back to the kitchen and see to the rest of it. *You'd* better get ready for your guests." Brooke giggled and then winked. "Knock 'em dead." She sped off before Faith could reply.

Eager to prove Wolfe's trust in her was not misplaced, Faith returned to the library. She had made up a packet of information for the Drelincourts about the history of their collection and the estimated value of each book based on prior sales. It was only a starting place, of course, but at least they would know she had a reasonable basis for her offer.

Faith sat down at her desk and opened the document on her computer. Before she did anything else, she gave it a final read, making sure no embarrassing typos had escaped her the day before. Satisfied, she clicked the print icon and requested fourteen copies, eleven for their guests, one for herself, one for Wolfe if he was able to attend the negotiations, and one for Marlene should she decide to sit in.

Not that the assistant manager had any reason to. Faith closed her eyes. She didn't want to think about what it would be like to try to appear competent and professional during the meeting while Marlene stared at her disapprovingly. Faith couldn't blame Laura for being nervous around the woman, but she wasn't going to let Marlene spoil this either, especially not for Wolfe. She was going to do exactly as he had suggested—knock 'em dead.

Before all fourteen copies had finished printing, Laura came into the library, cleaned up and ready to work. "Um, I guess I don't really know what a library assistant does."

"Technically? Assist the librarian." Faith gave her an encouraging nod. "You're going to help me do whatever needs doing around here. And along the way I'll explain the kinds of things I usually do and how they're done. How does that sound?"

"Wonderful."

The hum and whir of the printer stopped abruptly, and Faith picked up the still-warm sheets of paper from the tray. "Your first assignment is to separate these into fourteen sets, three-hole-punch them, and then put each one into a binder. The punch and the binders are in that cabinet."

She pointed to the gorgeous antique bombé chest near the desk, thinking as she always did that it was a crime to use it for something as mundane as office supplies. Laura retrieved the necessary items, and Faith handed her the reports.

For several minutes there was only the squeak and crunch of the hole punch and the shuffling of pages as Faith reviewed the financial information she and Wolfe had discussed previously, information she would not be sharing with the prospective sellers. Then she realized Laura had stopped. "Something wrong?"

Laura shook her head, staring at one of the pages she had just punched. "These books sure are worth a lot of money. I could get my degree for what just a few of these cost."

"Amazing, isn't it? But when you think that Agatha Christie herself signed each of them, some of them nearly a hundred years ago, it makes them pretty special." She studied Laura's eager face for a moment. "So what *about* that degree? If you're serious about doing library work for real, you'll have to get one."

"Oh, I am." Her cheeks turned a little pink. "I haven't had time to do more than take a few basic courses at the community college, but I'm going to try to take more this coming semester." She sighed. "Even if I take a class every semester from now on, including summer school, do you know how old I'll be before I get my degree?"

"And how old will you be by then if you don't get your degree?"

A shy, crooked smile touched Laura's lips. "Now you sound like my aunt. She's the one who told me I ought to take some courses whenever I could."

"She sounds like a smart lady. When was the last time you took a course for credit?"

Laura fiddled with the edge of the report she held. "It's been a while. Two or three years ago, I think, but I have enough money saved to take some more. When you got Ms. Russell to agree to let me work with you for a while, it made me really excited about eventually returning to school."

"I hope you do. Meanwhile, we'll see you get some practical experience."

Once the reports were finished and everything was ready for the arrival of the Drelincourt family, Faith spent the remainder of the afternoon showing Laura where things were shelved and how they were organized. Then they reshelved the books that had been returned that morning.

They were just about to stop for something to eat when Faith's cell phone rang.

"It's Marlene," Faith said when she saw the display.

Laura bit her lip and clutched a stack of books against herself.

Faith answered the call. "Marlene, what's happening?"

"The first of the Drelincourts have pulled up in front. Come out and greet them."

"I'll be right there." Faith felt the slightest tingle of excitement and panic run through her as she ended the call. It was time.

She smiled at Laura, more to steady herself than her new assistant. Attitude was half the battle, right? "I'm off to meet our guests. Are you all through?"

Laura set the reports in a neat stack on the corner of the desk. "Yes. Are they the way you want them?"

"They're perfect." Faith beamed at her. "Thank you. Now if you'll put everything back where you got it from, we're good for the day."

"Thanks for giving me a chance." Laura picked up the hole punch, and her expression became earnest. "I promise I can do this."

"I know you can." Faith glanced at the antique clock on the library's wide mantel. "Now go home and have a good evening, and we'll see what we need to tackle tomorrow, all right?"

Laura nodded. "And you can tell me all about the Drelincourt cousins and their uncle. Do you think they're terribly rich?"

Faith shrugged. "I suppose they must be reasonably well-off if the grandfather was a noted investor, but sometimes the second and third generations don't end up with much. It depends on how smart they were with their money over the years. Of course, if they can afford to book the manor for their reunion, they must be doing fine."

"Must be nice to not have to wonder where the money's coming from."

"Or maybe that's why they're interested in selling their Christie collection. I guess we'll find out."

Maxwell Drelincourt was well named. He was a stately, silver-haired man who would not have looked out of place in a boardroom, a courtroom, or any of the palaces of Europe. Still, he wasn't as richly dressed as Faith had expected. His dark suit was of excellent quality and carefully pressed, but it was hardly new. She could tell from the lines at the corners of his eyes and in his cheeks as well as from the warmth in his expression that he was a kindly man.

"This is Faith Newberry, our librarian," Marlene told him.

Faith held out her hand. "Good evening, Mr. Drelincourt. It's so good to have you here."

He clasped her hand and bowed slightly over it. "It's good to be here again," he said, then introduced the young woman standing beside him as his niece Tilly.

She had the same gentility her uncle displayed, along with his dark eyes and tall frame. Her simple, calf-length dress was a lovely shade of plum, reflecting her uncle's quiet elegance. Faith thought Tilly must be in her early twenties, though she seemed to have the gravity and maturity of someone much older, and her expression was alert and intelligent. But she, too, smiled warmly and shook Faith's hand.

"We were here two years ago for the Agatha Christie retreat," Tilly remarked. "Uncle Max thought it would be a brilliant place to have our family reunion."

He nodded. "We both remember you had quite a fine library."

"We're hoping it will be even finer by the time you and your family leave," Faith said with a smile.

Mr. Drelincourt shook a finger at her. "We'll have to see about that, young lady. Our books have been in the family some time now, and you're going to have to make us an extremely attractive offer before we'll be willing to let them go."

"Uncle Max, you promised we'd leave the business talk until tomorrow," Tilly said. "Tonight we're supposed to relax and spend time with the family."

Mr. Drelincourt laughed. "Yes, I know." He tucked her arm through his. "Tilly always looks after me, Ms. Newberry."

"And you always look after me," Tilly told him.

"And spoil you rotten."

She grinned. "That too."

Faith chuckled. "I think I'm going to enjoy getting to know all of you." *And those first editions.*

"Ms. Russell tells me we're the first to arrive," he said. "If you don't mind, I'd love to see that library. I remember you had some wonderful early editions of the Brontës' works and an illustrated—"

"Now, Uncle Max, I thought you were going to rest for a while before dinner," Tilly said, not quite severe.

"Are you misbehaving again?" A woman much nearer to forty than thirty, bundled in a full-length cashmere coat and wearing the most gorgeous stiletto-heeled boots Faith had ever seen, strode up to Mr. Drelincourt.

His face lit. "Michelle, darling, it's so good to see you!"

She returned his hug, kissed the air next to his cheek, then did the same to Tilly. "Oh, this weather. I flew straight into Logan from my conference in LA, and I was afraid we weren't going to be able to land. Then I thought the cab wasn't going to get here. I asked my admin to get me a car, but the woman at the desk told me I didn't have a reservation. I didn't have time to hash it out with her right then."

"I'm glad you made it," her uncle said. "I hope none of the

others will have any trouble." He turned to Faith and Marlene. "This is my niece Michelle Foxe."

"Michelle Drelincourt," she said, shaking hands with both of them. "I haven't been Foxe for years now, Uncle Max."

"Sorry, dear. Old habits, you know."

"It's good to have you here, Ms. Drelincourt," Faith said.

She shook her head, making her long earrings jingle. "You're going to have a lot of Drelincourts to keep up with. You might as well call us by our first names. I'm Michelle."

Faith smiled. "I'm Faith, the librarian here, and this is Marlene, the assistant manager."

"Hello," Marlene said, clearly unsure whether to admire the woman or envy her. Michelle was even more perfectly put together than Marlene.

Faith's train of thought was interrupted by the insistent yipping of a small dog—a Chihuahua, if Faith had to guess—and she was glad her cat, Watson, was safely at home. He took particular pleasure in teasing the tiny things.

A tall man in a heavy coat with a fur-trimmed hood walked in. He was followed by a woman who, despite her long wool jacket, was a shorter, bonier version of Michelle. The woman's yipping dog strained against the leash, desperate to get at whatever the man behind her had in a zebra-striped pet carrier.

"Nadine," the man with the carrier pled, concern in his faded blue eyes, "can't you keep him quiet for even half a minute?"

"You know," the first man purred with a feral flash of white teeth, "in Greenland they wouldn't have much use for a dog like that. He couldn't even pull a bread basket."

The woman snatched the small dog off the floor. "Don't you listen to that Neanderthal, Mr. Darcy. You don't need to work for a living."

Momentarily distracted, the dog licked her face, and the second man smirked.

"Don't laugh." The first man gestured toward the carrier. "That little speck wouldn't even make a good foot warmer."

"Here's more of our cheery crew," Michelle said as the three newcomers approached. "My sister, Nadine, and Uncle Jeff's boys, Derek and Eric. No, they're not twins."

The two men glared at Michelle.

"Welcome to Castleton Manor. I'm Marlene Russell, the assistant manager. If there's anything you need during your stay, please let me know. This is Faith Newberry, our librarian."

Derek raised one eyebrow. "Ah, so you're the one who wants to spirit away our collection of Dame Agatha's work."

Faith shook his hand. He reminded her of a panther—smooth and stealthy. "I'm certainly going to try." She turned to Nadine and her dog. "So this is Mr. Darcy. He's darling. I'm so glad you brought him. We specialize in pampering pets at the manor. And who do you have there?"

Eric held up the carrier.

Faith peeked inside. For a moment she thought it was empty, but then a pair of baby-blue eyes blinked at her, and she realized there was a tiny black kitten huddled in the carrier's back corner.

"That's Donnie," Eric said. "Well, Don Quixote, but he's still kind of little to fit the name."

"Oh, my goodness, he's precious," Faith said. "When he's not so scared, I'd love to get to know him."

"It's a deal." Eric smiled.

By then Derek and Nadine were talking to Tilly and Mr. Drelincourt. Eric and Michelle joined them, the six of them talking over each other.

"It's starting to sound like a family reunion already," Faith said, laughing.

Marlene nodded. "And that's only half of them."

Faith turned. "Not for long."

A stoop-shouldered man came toward them. His thinning hair was reddish rather than dark like the rest of the family's, and he squinted at them through his thick glasses.

"I guess I found the right place." The man shook the snow off his coat and folded it over one arm. "How is everyone? Uncle Max." He hugged Mr. Drelincourt and kissed Michelle, Nadine, and Tilly.

"A handshake will do for me," Derek said, suiting the action to the word. "Ms. Russell and Ms. Newberry, this is our oldest brother, Lloyd. We've got another brother and a sister too, who'll be here if the storm doesn't hit. Lloyd, Ms. Newberry wants our books."

"Please call me Faith." She shook his hand.

"I suppose we'll all get to know each other well over the next few days," Michelle said. "I understand there won't be any other guests."

"Not until our next retreat, which is more than a week away," Marlene told her.

"Making sure that all of us stay out of trouble will keep you busy." Michelle glanced over her shoulder at the sound of the door opening and closing and low chatter from the entrance. She beamed at one of the three men who had just come in. "Speaking of trouble," she said loud enough for him to hear, "Skip!"

The man had intensely blue eyes and short, spiky dark hair with bleached tips. "Tilly!" He rushed toward Michelle and then did a comical double take. "No, wait a minute. That couldn't be Michelle, could it? How is it you never look a day older?"

Mr. Drelincourt chuckled, and Tilly rolled her eyes.

"Liar," Michelle grumbled, but there was a smile behind the grumbling. "And how's Pongo there?"

Skip shook his head and gave the short-haired mutt at his feet a pat. "You know good and well it's Petie. Petie, say hello."

The dog rose on his hind legs and gave a single bark.

That set the little Chihuahua off until Nadine managed to shush him.

Marlene introduced herself and Faith once more.

The second of the three latest arrivals, a sleekly fit man who might have been former military, maybe law enforcement, shook hands with them. "Rob Drelincourt, ladies. Pleasure to meet you both. I guess you've met everybody but John here. And Ahnold."

Faith giggled at the heavy accent he used to pronounce the dog's name.

John was tall and lanky, and he gave Faith an uncertain smile that couldn't quite overcome what seemed to be perpetual weariness on his thin face. The German shepherd at his feet had a little stuffed brown corduroy cow in his mouth.

Skip looked up the sweeping staircases that led to the second floor. "Nice place. Ought to be room enough for all of us, eh, John? Better than three or four of us sharing the pullout couch in the playroom at Grandma's." He elbowed his cousin in the ribs.

John shrugged. "Nobody minded back then. It was like camping out."

Skip took off his coat, revealing an open Hawaiian shirt over a hot-pink T-shirt with a beer advertisement on it. "Well, Petie and I want our own room, right, boy?"

The little mixed-breed canine gave him a doggy smile, mouth wide and tongue lolling.

"You each have your own room," Marlene said, perusing her list. "But there's someone missing, isn't there?"

"Alice." Tilly turned toward the door, brow wrinkled. "I hope she isn't delayed too long."

Skip made a face. "I'm surprised old Davy-boy let her out from under his thumb even for a few days."

Derek scowled at him, Nadine pursed her thin lips, and Tilly's forehead puckered even more.

"Now don't worry, sweetie." Mr. Drelincourt put his arm around Tilly. "I'm sure she'll be here soon."

"Is Alice your sister?" Faith asked Tilly. "I guess I'm not sure who belongs to who."

"My cousin."

"Let's see," Michelle said. "There's me and Nadine and John. Our father was Conrad Drelincourt, the oldest. Then there was Uncle Jeff who had Lloyd, Rob, Eric, Derek, and Alice. Uncle Max didn't have any kids, so he keeps track of all of us. And then Aunt Georgie had Skip and Tilly. Clear enough?"

"I'll try to keep it straight," Faith promised.

Marlene addressed the family. "I'm sorry Mrs. Wexford seems to have been delayed. If you'd like to check in, I'll be happy to show you to your rooms so you can get settled before dinner is served. Your luggage has already been taken up. Or if you'd prefer, feel free to explore the manor. The pool and the stables are closed for the season, but the spas are open, one for people and one for pets. There's a billiard room, a music room, and a craft room. And of course, the library is at your disposal. Faith will be happy to give you a tour, or you can visit at your leisure."

The ten guests moved in a chattering mass to the front desk.

"I hope Alice is all right," Tilly said as she waited to register.

"I suppose she won't be bringing her husband with her," Faith said.

Tilly shook her head. "Uncle Max wanted it to be just us. He wants us to make our own decisions about whether or not we want to sell the books without any interference from spouses or significant others."

"I see," Faith said. It was unusual, but this was Mr. Drelincourt's party. "That does simplify things."

"Alice and John are both married," Michelle said. "Lloyd for the third time."

Lloyd didn't react. He seemed like someone who was always in control.

"Eric's technically married," Michelle went on, "though probably not for much longer. Rob's a widower."

Faith shot a quick look at him. He had that lean, muscular build that many police and firefighters had. *He must work out.*

Michelle didn't stop to take a breath. "Skip never could keep a girlfriend for more than a couple of months. Derek probably has girlfriends all over Europe, Africa, and Asia, but he doesn't tell us anything about them. And Nadine and Tilly are old maids."

Eric, Skip, and Derek seemed mildly annoyed, and again Tilly rolled her eyes.

Nadine said primly, "If I were to marry, I'd at least know how to keep my vows."

Michelle still smiled—she was clearly a cool customer—but her eyes turned hard.

Before Michelle could reply, Mr. Drelincourt slipped his arm around her. "Now, girls, I'm sure Faith doesn't want to hear about all the Drelincourt ups and downs, unless it has to do with our Christie collection."

Faith smiled. "I am most certainly interested in those. I understand your father—" She broke off when something small and dark shot across the floor, stopping all the chatter and setting the dogs off.

A tabby cat—back arched and snow-soaked fur on end—hissed and took refuge behind a potted plant in one corner.

"Lucy!" A round-faced young woman as wet and bedraggled as the cat hurried into the lobby, her dark eyes big and anxious, her overpermed hair pulled back from her face in a swiftly deteriorating bun. Seeing all eyes on her, she froze. Then she smiled faintly. "I'm so sorry. I'm afraid my cat got loose, and I don't—Lucy! There you are." Steering clear of the dogs, she rushed over to the plant and got down on her hands and knees. "Come on, sweetie. It's all right. Come on."

The cat gave a mournful meow.

The woman reached one hand toward it. "Come on, Lucy."

The cat leaned slightly toward her, sniffing her fingers, and the woman seized her. The feline meowed again, nudged open her coat, and slipped inside. The woman cuddled the cat against her, making little soothing sounds. "Sorry, everyone. It's been that kind of day. Hello, Uncle Max."

"Alice." Mr. Drelincourt put his arm around her, careful not to frighten the cat. "We were worried about you, honey. Is everything all right?"

Alice nodded, then pressed closer to him. "I probably should have left Lucy at home, but I didn't want—" She shrugged, a faint, tight smile touching her lips. "I thought she'd like a vacation. I guess I was wrong."

"You know the menagerie we have at home, kid," Rob told her. "With two boys, three dogs, two cats, a parrot, a hamster, and five goldfish, *I* was the one who needed a vacation, and the boys are happy to have their grandma spoil them for a few days."

Alice giggled and seemed to relax. "I hope you weren't waiting for me. I thought you'd be having dinner by now."

"Just getting registered," Mr. Drelincourt assured her. "You're right on time."

Derek snorted. "Now we can finally take care of this book business once and for all. I say sell the lot of them and get on with it."

"Now, not so fast," Lloyd began.

"Yeah," Rob said, "we're supposed to talk this out before we decide anything."

Once more, they began talking at the same time. Alice remained next to her uncle, her head down, her arms tight around her cat.

Faith glanced at Marlene, not sure if she should say something.

"All right!" Mr. Drelincourt's upraised hand restored calm.

The chatter stopped.

"As has already been mentioned," he said, "nothing has been settled yet. We have a great deal to talk over, about the books and about the family, and there are better places to do that than right here."

Alice's expression was one of almost pitiful gratitude. The rest of Mr. Drelincourt's nieces and nephews glanced at one another a little sheepishly and nodded.

"I was planning on us getting together tomorrow sometime before lunch to view your book collection. How about ten thirty in the library?" Faith suggested.

There was a general murmur of agreement from the cousins.

"Good." Faith smiled. "I'm so happy to have met all of you, and I can't wait to see those first editions."

"I'll get Mrs. Wexford checked in," Marlene said, "and then you can all get settled in your rooms and relax for a while. The kitchen has something wonderful planned for dinner, so we'll see you in the banquet hall at seven o'clock."

The guests seemed pleased at the prospect, and as soon as Alice had her room key, Marlene led them to the grand stairway and up to the second floor.

"This isn't going to be like trying to herd cats," Faith murmured as she watched them ascend. "More like juggling them."

4

The menu that night featured Cabernet-glazed filet mignon, which Faith knew was Brooke's own recipe, with baked potato and asparagus Parmigiano-Reggiano. There were artichoke-and-goat-cheese bruschetta, shrimp cocktail, and Caesar salad before the main course.

By the time they got to dessert, the Drelincourts had settled into what Faith imagined was usual for them—a lot of squabbling, a few barbed comments here and there, but mostly good-natured bantering and fond reminiscences. The crostini were never missed.

Faith accepted their invitation to join them for coffee and molten chocolate cake with black cherry sauce. "Provided," she insisted, "that we leave the business talk till tomorrow."

"No business talk," Mr. Drelincourt assured her. "Though I'm sure we'd all like to get to know you a bit. We wouldn't want the Christie collection going to anyone who wouldn't treat it right."

"Yeah," Rob said from the seat he had taken next to her. "Tell us about yourself. Having responsibility for a library like this must be pretty interesting work, especially with the literary events you host."

Faith told them about her work as librarian and archivist at Hawarden University and her decision to get away from the big city and come to live and work in Lighthouse Bay. She also told them about her stub-tailed tuxedo cat, Watson, making them laugh at some of his more outrageous antics. "You don't know how nice it was to find a job where I could bring him to work with me when I wanted to. And he certainly enjoys exploring the manor and snooping on the guests."

Nadine sat upright and picked up her Chihuahua from the chair next to her. "He's not in the manor now, is he? Mr. Darcy is easily upset, especially by cats."

The little dog yipped at the mention of his name and wriggled until Nadine put him down again.

"He's safely at home right now," Faith said, hoping that was true. Watson tended to go where he wanted. "I live in what used to be the gardener's cottage here on the grounds. But he often comes over to the manor or plays out in the gardens. He's a little tease sometimes, but he wouldn't do anything to hurt Mr. Darcy."

"He wouldn't mess with Ahnold more than once," John said, patting the German shepherd lying with his head on his master's shoe. This time the dog had brought along a worn, loosely stuffed pink pig.

"A hundred pounds' worth of dumb if you ask me," Derek scoffed.

"He's extremely intelligent. Watch." John held his hand out to his dog, who dropped the pig into it, and then pointed at the door. "Go out."

Ahnold happily trotted out into the corridor.

"Shut it," John said, and the dog nudged the door closed. "Okay, hide this wherever you want." He handed the pig to Derek.

Derek rolled his eyes, then scanned the room, finally settling on a small wicker basket on the corner of the table. He put the pig inside and replaced the lid. "I'll give him three minutes," he said as he walked over to the door and opened it. "Three."

"Come on," John said as the dog bounded inside, grinning at the expected game. "Ahnold, find it. Find the piggy."

The German shepherd lifted his head, sniffing the air, and padded over to the far side of the room.

Derek smirked.

"Find it," John urged.

Derek's smirk turned sour as Ahnold made a beeline for the table, pulled the lid off the wicker basket, and snapped up the stuffed pig.

"Good boy," John said, giving him a treat from his pocket and a pat on the head.

Skip snorted. "Ahnold's a big cream puff. It's the little mutts you have to worry about. Isn't that right, Petie? Sic 'em! Go on, sic 'em."

Petie responded with a happy woof, and everyone laughed.

Skip looked at him with mild disgust. "Some tough guy you are. You know, we were in Vegas a couple of months ago and—"

With a moaning howl of wind, the room went dark.

Several people gasped, and the Chihuahua whined from the other side of the table.

"Everybody, stay where you are," Faith said, managing to sound calmer than she felt. "It sounds like the storm put the power out. It should take only a moment or two for the generator to kick in. Hang on."

"Poor Lucy," Alice said from her place next to her uncle. "She'll be scared up in my room by herself." Clearly Alice was the one who was frightened.

"I'm sure she's fine," Faith said. "Cats usually don't mind—"

The lights flickered and then blazed back on.

Alice let out a sigh of relief. "I think I'd better go check on Lucy." She hurried away as fast as her plump legs could carry her.

"She shouldn't have brought that cat," Nadine said. "Not if it's just going to sit huddled in her room all the time. It might as well have stayed curled up at home, if you ask me."

"That's *if* anyone were to ask you, of course," Michelle said sweetly.

Faith looked from one sister to the other. There was definitely a story there, but she reminded herself that whatever the story was, it was none of her business.

"I think Alice's husband doesn't much like cats," Tilly confided to Faith.

Several minutes later Marlene came into the room. "I'm so sorry, everyone. The landlines and Internet services are down, but cell phones still work. As you know, the power went out, so we're running on the generator. But even if we get snowed in, it'll keep things going for a good long while. If that goes out for some reason, we have stacks of firewood, plenty of candles, and a full pantry."

Alice returned and announced, "Lucy's sound asleep."

"Do you think you should check on your little one?" Faith asked Eric, who had been sitting quietly through everything.

He patted the bulge in his large shirt pocket. "Donnie slept through the whole thing."

"Aww. He sleeps in your pocket?"

Eric shrugged rather sheepishly. "I got him when he still had to be bottle-fed. He doesn't like to be away from me. I only put him in the carrier because we had to fly."

Michelle raised one carefully penciled eyebrow. "And what are you going to do with him when he's too big for your pocket?"

"Get a bigger pocket."

Rob laughed and swatted his shoulder. "Does he get in the way of you playing pool?"

"I understand it's billiards here." Lloyd pushed his glasses up higher on his nose. "I'd sure like to give it a go."

"Pool, billiards, whatever," Rob said. "Come on and play. What do you say, Eric? It's early yet. Anyone else?" He looked appealingly at Faith.

She was surprised to feel her cheeks turn a little warm. He was only being friendly, she knew, but he was an attractive man in an all-American way. Still, she shook her head.

"I haven't played in years," John said, "but I wouldn't mind trying again. If the Wi-Fi is out and everything, I guess there's not much else to do for the night."

"How am I going to update my fantasy league?" Skip peered at his phone and sighed. "Anyone want to play some poker?"

Derek smirked at him. "Better than doing nothing, I suppose."

"Do you want to come watch us, Uncle Max?" Tilly asked. "I'm going to play billiards."

Her uncle shook his head, smiling. "I think I'll turn in for the night. It's been a long day getting here, and I think I'll just read for a while and then go to sleep."

She slipped her arm through his. "I'll go up with you and make sure you have everything you need."

"If you insist," he said fondly. "Good night, everyone. Faith, it was good to meet you, and I'm eager to talk about the collection."

"I'm eager to see the books," Faith replied honestly.

"Tomorrow, then," he said, and he and Tilly went up the stairs followed by a chorus of good nights from the rest of the family.

"You're welcome to join us in the billiard room," Rob told Faith.

She wavered.

"Come on," he urged, his gray eyes warm. "It'll be fun."

"Thank you," Faith replied, "but I won't be able to stay long. Watson is going to be mad enough as it is. He has crunchies all day, of course, but he's made it abundantly clear that those are no substitute for a proper meal served on time."

Alice gave Nadine and Michelle a tentative smile. "I'd love to catch up with you two."

The sisters looked warily at each other, and then Michelle nodded. "It has been a while."

"All right," Nadine said, with only a slight stiffness in her voice. She cradled her Chihuahua closer.

Faith opened the door that led from the banquet hall to the billiard room and turned on the lights. "Please make yourselves comfortable. The cues and balls are in the cabinet, and there are several decks of cards and other games in the drawer in the card table. And there's comfortable seating in the corner if you want to sit and visit."

Soon there was a lively poker game in progress, and John, apparently realizing in just a few minutes that he was not well suited to billiards, parked Ahnold and his pig next to Petie under the card table and joined in. Tilly had come back downstairs and took his place playing billiards. The three other women were settled in the corner, where Alice was telling Michelle and Nadine about Lucy.

That won't last long, Faith thought, judging by the growing impatience on the sisters' faces. Despite Rob's insistence that everyone was just starting to have fun, it was as good a time as any for her to say good night and return home to Watson. It had been a long day.

When she entered the lobby, she was surprised to see two men at the front desk, both of them white with snow. Marlene was checking them in.

"Marlene," Faith said, going over to the desk, "I thought you'd gone home a while ago."

"I decided I'd better stay the night. Have you looked outside?"

One of the newcomers, a short, squat man with a bulldog jaw, grinned at Faith. "It's really coming down now, ma'am. We lost control of our car out there on the highway and had to walk up here. It's a wonder we weren't frozen solid, right, Gordo?"

His companion, a thin young man with a wispy brown mustache, nodded.

"We're hosting a private function at present," Marlene said, with just a touch of severity in her tone, "so we hope you understand that certain areas of the manor will be unavailable to you."

The first man shrugged. "That's all right. So long as it's warm and there's something to eat, we're good."

"I'll show you to your rooms then. Faith, you stay," Marlene said. "I'll be right back."

Faith glanced at the clock over the desk, trying not to be obvious. It was still relatively early. "No problem."

The heavyset man nodded at her, and she was sure if he'd been wearing anything but a knit cap, he would have tipped it. "Ma'am."

"Good night," she told both men.

"I gave them a couple of rooms as far away from the Drelincourts as I could," Marlene said when she returned. "I don't know if either of them has ever stayed in anything more luxurious than a chain motel off the highway."

Faith smiled. "You couldn't very well turn them out on a night like this."

"No, I know that. I just hope the weather clears and they can be on their way tomorrow. Though if their car's off the road in a snowdrift, it may take a while to get it up and running again."

"You can handle it, no matter what happens," Faith assured her. "I hope Brooke got home safely. I think she made a great impression with that dinner."

"She should have stayed tonight."

Faith nodded. "Well, I should go home. Watson hasn't had his dinner yet."

"You'd better take one of the rooms," Marlene said.

Faith almost did a double take. Marlene was concerned about her? "Thank you, but—"

"We wouldn't want you to miss your meeting with the Drelincourts tomorrow morning."

Faith stifled a laugh. The Drelincourts. That also explained Marlene's concern for Brooke. Who would cook for their special guests if she wasn't here, with the head chef on vacation? "Don't worry. I'll be back in the morning since I don't have to drive."

Faith bundled up as snugly as she could and managed to break a trail back to the cottage. It wasn't far, just through the now-bare Victorian garden on the manor grounds, but by the time she reached her front door, she was freezing and covered with snow. As she had hoped, Watson was waiting for her.

He was stretching on the sofa, no doubt having napped there most of the day. Then he came and sat expectantly at her feet, his black-and-white fur neatly groomed as if he were ready for some formal occasion.

"Yes sir," she said, smiling as she unbundled herself, relieved to feel warm again. "Your table will be ready in a moment."

Watson gave her a disapproving meow and twitched his stubby tail.

"All right. I don't suppose you'd let me take time to build a fire before you eat. No?"

He huffed.

"Fine. I guess you have been neglected all day." She hung her wraps near the blazeless hearth and then headed into the kitchen.

Watson made expectant little half-purring mews as he trotted ahead of her, glancing back frequently to see if she was still coming.

After Faith filled his food bowl and gave him fresh water, she went to the hearth. "Are you interested in what I have in my pocket?" she called.

There was no response from the kitchen until she unwrapped the surprise. Immediately, Watson was at her feet. Since she had known beforehand that the day was likely to be a long one, she had stopped at the pet spa in the manor on her lunch break to pick up some tunaroons, a specialty of the Happy Tails Gourmet Bakery and Watson's favorite treat.

"Well, come on then."

He galloped back into the kitchen.

Faith put a tuna-flavored macaroon in his bowl. "How's that?" she said, stroking his silky back.

As she'd expected, now that he had his treat he made no acknowledgment of her presence.

She went into the living room once more and laid a roaring fire. Her face and hands were thawed by the time it was burning well, but her feet were still freezing. The only thing to do was soak in a warm bath, then slip into the warmest, softest flannel pajamas she had. Tomorrow was bound to be a challenging day, no matter how well she had prepared for it. The storm was another unexpected addition to the list of challenges she had to deal with, like the arrival of those two men tonight.

Marlene was probably right about their being out of place at the manor. She couldn't imagine what they were doing in Lighthouse Bay. Maybe they were just passing through. They were definitely unlike any of the manor's usual bookish guests, but they wouldn't be around long. Not if Marlene had anything to say about it. But that was Marlene's problem, not Faith's.

Once she had bathed and gotten ready for bed, Faith reviewed her evening with the Drelincourts and realized it had gone amazingly well. Despite a bit of friction and a few precisely aimed barbs, there had been no actual name-calling between the cousins, no fisticuffs, and no one had stormed out of the manor, refusing to return.

Now if she could only get them to behave as nicely during negotiations, this whole endeavor would be a success. She couldn't wait to see that complete set of autographed first editions all laid out on the table in the library tomorrow morning. The idea that some of them were nearly one hundred years old and had been signed by Dame Agatha herself made Faith's librarian's heart beat a little faster. Or maybe that had been caused by Rob Drelincourt's appealing smile, she indulged herself.

"It's going to be a fantastic day," she told Watson as she curled up beside him under her flannel sheets, and then she fell asleep.

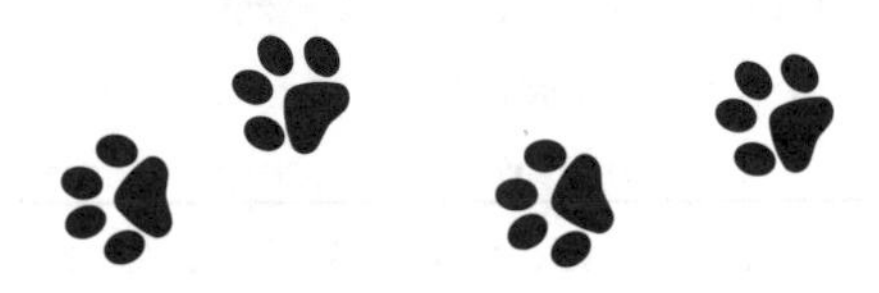

The snow was still pelting down on Lighthouse Bay when Faith trekked to the manor the next morning. Bundled up as she was, it was awkward enough trying to get down what she hoped was the path through the garden and up to the house without having an armload of squirming cat to carry.

"Maybe you should lay off the tunaroons for a few days, Rumpy."

Watson grumbled from under her coat. He'd never liked his nickname.

"I want you to be on your best behavior," she told him. "There are three dogs and two cats visiting, and I don't want you teasing any of them. Do you understand?"

He didn't respond.

"And you're to leave the Chihuahua strictly alone."

He huffed.

"One of the cats is a pretty little tabby called Lucy," she added in a singsong voice.

She glanced down into her coat and saw two suddenly interested green eyes turned up to her.

"Behave yourself, and I'm sure you'll get to meet her."

She trudged a little farther and shifted the cat up a little higher, wishing the path she had broken through the snow last night was still there. She needed to get into the manor and make herself at least somewhat presentable before she met with the Drelincourts at ten thirty. Hauling fifty pounds of grouchy cat around through a snowstorm certainly wasn't going to give her that professional, put-together look.

Maybe fifty pounds was the tiniest bit of an exaggeration, but she was glad when they finally reached the manor and she could set him down.

Watson arched his back, stretching himself from end to end, and sauntered off, stopping occasionally to take in the intriguing smells of their new guests. Halfway to the stairs, he made an emergency stop to groom his left front paw before continuing on his way.

"Remember what I said," she called after him.

As always, he made no indication that he had heard her.

"I guess there was no chance you'd keep him at home today."

Faith forced her expression into pleasant lines before she turned. "Good morning, Marlene. You know that even if I had left him at home there was no guarantee he'd stay. But in this weather, I didn't want to take a chance that I'd get stuck here and he'd be on his own at the cottage for a couple of days. My only other option was to stay home with him, and you know today's meeting is too important for that."

"Far too important," Marlene said, her mouth in a taut smile. "He'd better not annoy any of the Drelincourts' pets. I have enough trouble trying to make sure those drifters who came in last night aren't an embarrassment to the manor."

"Drifters?" Faith barely managed not to laugh. "They're not that bad."

"They wouldn't be that bad if they'd stay in their rooms, but Laura told me she saw them roaming around upstairs this morning while everyone else was at breakfast. And I noticed the big one, Morris, poking around by the storage room near Mr. Drelincourt's room. He claimed he was looking for the ice machine."

"I guess that's not unreasonable if he's never stayed somewhere like this before."

"I reminded him that the end of the floor was off-limits to anyone but the Drelincourt party."

"Well, I'll tell that to Watson," Faith said, "but you know he has selective hearing."

Marlene frowned.

"Come on," Faith said. "You don't think they're here to steal things, do you?"

"Castleton Manor is full of priceless items. I don't know why someone of that inclination wouldn't want to take them."

"If that's the case, I think it's a pretty bad plan. Going out in a snowstorm and getting stranded and just hoping you'll be close enough to take refuge somewhere that has a lot of valuables? Even criminals aren't usually that dumb."

"Maybe. But keep your eyes open. It doesn't help that we have more unexpected visitors."

"We do?"

Her mouth in a prim line, Marlene jerked her chin toward the woman who was coming down the stairs and smiling at Faith.

"Aunt Eileen!"

"This is supposed to be the Drelincourt family reunion, not the Newberry one. Just don't get talking and be late for your meeting," Marlene said as she started to march off. "And keep that cat of yours out of trouble."

"What has the little rascal Watson been up to now?" Eileen asked. "Marlene seemed like her usual grumpy self."

Faith hurried across the lobby to her. "What in the world are you doing here? Wait. Let me get out of all this so I can hug you."

Faith stripped off the wool scarf, mittens, and cap Eileen had knitted for her, glad her aunt had seen how much she was enjoying them. Then as best she could, she brushed away the snow that clung to her coat and boots.

When she had all her things piled on a nearby chair, she was finally able to give her aunt an enormous hug. "What are you doing here? It's terrible outside."

Eileen flashed her warmest smile, her eyes sparkling. "I wasn't going to let a snowstorm keep me from seeing those Christie first editions. By the time I got to the manor, the weather was turning really bad, and I realized that going back home wasn't a good idea either. So here I am, waiting until things get better."

"I hope the Mustang is all right."

Eileen laughed. "That's why I didn't want to risk going back home. I'll probably be the last visitor you get today. Maybe for several days, judging by those storm clouds."

"The forecast isn't promising," Faith said. "We'll probably have a skeleton crew today, but we don't have many guests staying right now, so we should be fine. Just a family reunion and a couple of stragglers who got stranded in the storm last night."

"Yes." There was an eager light in Eileen's eyes that Faith knew must also be in her own. "The family with the Agatha Christie collection. Is it as good as they claim?"

"I haven't seen it yet," Faith admitted. "They just got in last night, and with there being eleven of them all told, it was a bit of a miracle they all got here without any real problems. Anyway, I'm supposed to meet with them at ten thirty." She glanced at her watch. "I need to get myself tidied up and head to the library. Would you . . . ?"

Eileen held up both hands. "Oh no. This is your party."

"But you're a librarian with much more experience than I have. You could give the meeting a certain gravitas that I—"

"Oh, stop. You know you're anxious to get started, and I know you'll do great. But if you want someone to come and *ooh* and *ahh* over the collection once the deal is made, you can count me in."

"I'll do that for sure." Faith hugged her aunt one more time. "I have to go. I'm glad you made it here in one piece."

"If I'm going to be stranded here for a while," Eileen said, "I hope we can make time for a little girl talk."

"Definitely. Unless I'm tied up with the Drelincourts, how about lunch?"

"No pressure," Eileen said. "I know you have business to see to. But if you're free, I'd love it."

"It's a date then. Sort of."

Faith hurried to the library and found a large table with fourteen comfortable chairs and a copy of the report about the valuation of the Christie collection set out at each place.

"Did I do it right?" Laura asked, her eyes eager. "I didn't know if you'd be able to get here before the meeting, so I thought I'd do what I could until you came. I hope I didn't do anything wrong."

Faith squeezed her arm. "Of course you didn't do anything wrong. It's just right, and now I can get myself put together before our guests arrive." She rummaged in her purse for her hand mirror and her makeup bag and began touching up. "It's pretty bad out there, isn't it?"

"Awful," Laura said, shaking her head. "I went to the Brontë Suite to look outside, and the road is totally packed with snow. I don't think anything can move."

"That's what I was afraid of. How are we doing for staff?"

"A few of the housekeepers made it in. Brooke too, but I don't think any of the kitchen help is here. Maybe one or two."

"We might all have to help peel potatoes."

Laura giggled. "At least we don't have a big retreat or anything. Just the Drelincourts and those two men who came last night. I don't think they'll give us much trouble."

"I'm sure we'll get through admirably." Faith put on a touch more lipstick and decided that was all she needed.

"Do you want me to bring coffee or anything for the meeting?"

Faith started to accept, but then, remembering what Marlene had said about spilling something on one of the first editions, she shook her head. "Lunch is supposed to be served as soon as we've finished."

"I'll see if Ms. Russell wants me to help in the kitchen."

"Good. And tell Brooke she did great on dinner last night. The Drelincourts were very impressed."

"I will." Laura gave her an encouraging smile. "I hope it goes great and you get to buy the books."

Once Laura was gone, Faith put her mirror and makeup bag back into her purse and then walked around the library table, taking one last look before the potential sellers started to arrive. She didn't know if Wolfe had returned to the manor before the weather got really bad. She didn't know if Marlene was going to come to the meeting.

She glanced at her watch. Eighteen minutes after ten. She still had twelve—

"Hey, Faith?"

Faith jumped and then turned to the door.

Skip walked about halfway into the room. "Did I scare you?" he asked with a grin.

"No, just surprised me, that's all."

He came over to the table, hands in the pockets of his baggy jeans. "I know I'm a little early, but I wanted to check out this great library Uncle Max has been telling us about." His gaze moved from the intricately woven Turkish carpet, up two levels of bookshelves to the richly colored fresco painted on the ceiling high above them, and then back down again. "This is pretty awesome. Nice place to work, I'd say."

"It's wonderful."

"The perfect place for a collection like ours," he said, still glancing around.

"I think so." Faith could tell there was something he wasn't saying. Was there a problem? "You didn't bring your books with you?"

Skip shrugged. "I'll get them when it's time. I wanted to peek in here first."

"Was there something you wanted to talk to me about?"

Again he shrugged. "Nothing important. I mean, I thought we were going to be the only ones here during the reunion. I heard some other people checked in last night."

"Oh. Just a couple of guys who got stuck on the road. They had to walk up to the manor. Their rooms are on the opposite end of the floor from yours and your family's. You probably won't see them much."

Skip ran one hand through his blond-tipped hair. "Good. I don't want Uncle Max being bothered by anyone. Did you notice what they were like?"

"I didn't pay much attention to them. A heavyset man. A young guy with a mustache. Do you know them?"

He chewed his lower lip. "The young guy, did he have brown hair?"

"I think so. Is there something wrong?" Faith asked.

He grinned suddenly. "Wrong? Nah. I just thought maybe they were a couple of guys I might have met in Vegas. You didn't happen to get their names, did you?"

She shook her head. "I don't remember. And I couldn't give them out anyway. That's one of our policies."

"Yeah, I understand. Privacy and all that. Gotcha." Skip didn't say anything else. He didn't turn to go. What exactly was he after?

"Do you spend a lot of time in Vegas?" Faith asked. "I've never been."

"Oh yeah. Great place. Lots of fun. Free food and booze. How can you go wrong?"

"Until you have to get back to making a living, right?"

"If you're into that sort of thing." Skip winked at her. "I'd rather see what comes next and take my chances."

She laughed. "I like having a little security."

"Security's overrated," he said. "Petie and I do just fine. You never know when you're going to win that big pot and be set for life."

"Or you might drive out there in a nice new Chevy and come back on a bus. That is, if you can still afford a ticket."

"I guess you never know." Skip gave her a look that said he'd heard that one a time or two. He stepped over to the window and pulled back the heavy curtain.

From where Faith stood, she could see nothing in the gray light outside but swirling snow. Even the cottage, close as it was, was no longer visible.

Skip's usually carefree expression was grim now. "I don't like being stuck here. Don't get me wrong. It's a nice place, but I don't like being cooped up. I want to sell these books and get out."

"I'll do my best," Faith assured him, "but that depends on whether you and the rest of your family come to an agreement about whether to sell and for how much." She checked her watch. There were five minutes left before the meeting. "It's almost time to start."

"Yeah." His habitual grin returned. "I left Petie on guard, but I'll go get him and my books and make sure everyone else is on the way."

"Thanks. I'll see you soon."

Skip sped out of the room.

"One of our Christie owners?" Wolfe asked, poking his head around the door. He was dressed more casually than he had been the day before, but he still looked as if he'd just stepped out of *GQ*. "There aren't any others I should watch out for now, are there?"

"I think the coast is clear. For the moment. You'd better come sit down so you'll be out of the heavy traffic areas." Faith pulled out the chair at the head of the long table.

But Wolfe took the chair to its right. "This is your show. Remember?"

She nodded. "I hope the collection is everything they claim. It's going to be pretty fabulous if it is."

He ruffled the pages of the report in front of him. "I take it this is the information we discussed earlier? Comparables? Recent sales?"

"I want them to know that should we make an offer, we didn't pull it out of thin air. And we have some basis for making adjustments depending on variables in the condition of the books."

Wolfe's eyes warmed with his smile. "I'd say we're ready to go. And right on time."

Faith looked up to see Mr. Drelincourt and Tilly at the library door, each of them carrying several carefully wrapped books.

"Mr. Drelincourt, good morning." Faith shook the man's hand and then his niece's. "Tilly, how are you?"

"Just fine." Tilly set down her books, then relieved her uncle of the ones he carried. "I could do without the weather, but this isn't a bad spot to be snowed in."

"Glad to hear you're not disappointed with the place," Wolfe said, standing and holding out his hand. "I'm Wolfe Jaxon, the owner of Castleton Manor. I've heard a lot about this collection of yours, and I'm eager to see it."

He shook hands with both of their guests, and they all sat down.

"As you may have heard," Mr. Drelincourt said, "all the Christie books were collected by my grandfather as they were released. My father always said my grandfather bought the first one in a train station because he'd forgotten to bring along the book he was reading at the time. He saw the next one in the bookstore and remembered how much he'd liked the first, so he bought that one too. After that, he had a standing order for her books. Sometime in the 1950s or '60s, when Dame Agatha was visiting her American publisher, he arranged to meet her and had her autograph all the books he had collected."

"Whoa," Wolfe said. "There must have been dozens of books by then."

Mr. Drelincourt smiled. "There were. But I think she was rather impressed with his interest in her stories. She was apparently a great sport about it, and after that he would always buy her most recent release and then mail it to her for her autograph. All but this one." He unwrapped the topmost volume on the stack of books, *Sleeping Murder: Miss Marple's Last Case.*

"Oh yes," Faith said, feeling a rush of excitement. "That one was published after her death. I suppose it couldn't be autographed."

"Well, yes and no," Mr. Drelincourt said with a touch of a smile, and he opened the front cover of the book. "When she sent back my grandfather's copy of *Curtain,* which was Poirot's last case, she had signed the book and put in this note."

There was a small slip of paper tucked inside the book jacket for *Sleeping Murder.* Faith was intrigued to see that it was Agatha Christie's own engraved notepaper with one line written on it: *In case I've missed one after all these years. Agatha Christie.* The name written on the note was larger than the rest of the writing. It was more than a signature. It was an autograph.

"Amazing," Wolfe said. "Just amazing." He reached out to touch it with one finger and then stopped himself.

"Oh, wait," Faith said, and she went to the bombé chest and removed a box of cotton gloves. "I meant to have these out for everyone to use. We want to be careful with such a special collection."

"Good idea," Nadine said, coming in with her own stack of wrapped books and Mr. Darcy on a leash at her heels. "I can't say I've ever thought these scrawlings were even close to being literature, but if they're valuable, then by all means, let's take care of them."

"This isn't your freshman lit class, Nadine dear." Michelle swept in after her, carrying more of the collection. "You're not going to impress us with those highbrow books you won't admit even you can't make sense out of. Give me a good story any day."

Nadine put her books on the table with the others.

Tilly glared at her. "They may not be the most profound

writings of the last century, but they're an awful lot of fun. I'd rather be snowed in with these than that mess *Ulysses*."

Nadine sniffed. "I can't help it if people don't take the trouble to understand genius." She arched an eyebrow at Michelle. "At least as much as they're able."

"I think Joyce was laughing up his sleeve at the whole literary world when he wrote that," Rob said as he, Derek, and Lloyd added their first editions to the ones on the table. "The emperor has no clothes, and all you highbrows are afraid to admit it." There was a touch of a sly smile on his face when his eyes met Faith's.

Wolfe went suddenly still beside her.

She smiled at Rob in return, careful to keep it strictly professional.

"Now, now," Mr. Drelincourt said mildly as the three men sat down. "We're talking about Christie, not James Joyce."

"Have they started up on him?" John said as he and Ahnold entered the library. "Not again. Please."

"We were just admiring *Sleeping Murder*," Faith said. "I'm eager to see *The Mysterious Affair at Styles*."

"Oh, that one's mine," Michelle said, unwrapping one volume with gloved hands. "Grandfather inherited them all from his father and left each of us our share, oldest to youngest, in order of publication. So I have the first, and Tilly has the last."

She opened the front cover, displaying the autograph in fading blue ink. There was a tiny blot on the initial letter *A*, but the signature was clear: *Agatha Christie*.

"Nice," Wolfe said, giving Faith a nod of approval.

"I understand you each have several of the books," Faith said.

"Yes," Michelle said, "except some of us have one more than the others, since the books couldn't be divided exactly evenly."

"Where's Skip?" John asked.

"He was in here a few minutes ago," Faith said, making a mental count. "He went back to his room for his books and to get Petie. Who are we missing?"

There were eight Drelincourts at this point. Who hadn't showed up yet?

"Eric," Derek said. "But he might have had a brilliant idea for one of his books and had to write it down before he forgot."

"He's an author?" Faith asked, impressed. "What sort of thing does he write?"

"Oh, sappy, depressing stuff," Derek replied. "The main character usually dies a slow and painful death from some disease."

"Alice isn't here yet," Tilly said.

Lloyd shrugged. "She's been running late since the day she was born."

"She was two weeks late even then," Rob said with a grin.

"I'm glad you two aren't *my* brothers," Tilly said.

"Don't be too smug," Derek told her. "You got stuck with Skip, wherever he is."

"Right here."

Everyone at the table turned to see Skip standing in the doorway with Alice and Eric behind him. They were empty-handed.

"All right," Skip said, approaching the table with Petie at his heel. "Whoever the prankster is, your little joke isn't funny."

"What do you mean?" his uncle asked. "Go get your books. We've got business to discuss."

"Uncle Max," Alice said, looking as if she might burst into tears, "they're gone."

6

"They're all gone," Alice said, her voice shaking. "Skip thinks somebody hid them for a joke. I don't know why any of you would do that. I can't—" She bit her lip, blinking hard. "I can't let anything happen to those books. David would never understand."

Faith glanced at Wolfe.

Wolfe gave her an almost imperceptible shrug in answer.

"Yours are missing too," Skip said to Eric. It wasn't a question.

Eric nodded. "When I went to get them out of my suitcase, they were gone, wrapping and all."

"Don Quixote's all right, isn't he?" Faith asked, and she was relieved when the tiny black kitten popped his head out of Eric's pocket.

"He's fine." Eric petted him absently. "I guess he's not much of a watchcat."

"Petie either," Skip said, scowling at the dog, who panted happily back at him.

"I couldn't tell if anything in my room was bothered," Alice said. "Lucy's been hiding under the bed since we got here. I don't know how anyone could have gotten into my things." She looked pleadingly at her family. "If anybody moved our books to be funny or something, please just say so. I promise we won't be mad."

"I will," Skip said. "I was counting on selling those stupid things. I mean it. It's not funny."

The seven cousins already at the table glanced at one another and at the three latecomers, all of them appearing perplexed and denying any knowledge of the missing books.

Alice began to cry in earnest now, Eric shook his head as if something like this always happened to him, and Skip continued to demand to know where his books were.

"Wait," Mr. Drelincourt said, his firm voice carrying over all the others.

The cousins quieted.

"You three sit down," Mr. Drelincourt said. "Let's figure this thing out."

Alice sat next to Rob, blotting her eyes with a tissue, and Eric sat on the other side of her, resignation in every line of his body.

Mouth taut, eyes hard, his hair sticking up like the quills on a porcupine, Skip paused. Then he dragged a chair back from the table and dropped into it. "What's to figure out? My books are gone. Somebody stole them. It's not brain surgery."

Mr. Drelincourt held up his hand, then regarded everyone at the table in turn. "First off, Alice is right. If anyone is hiding the books as a joke, now's the time to say so and be done with it. There's no use wasting Faith's time and Mr. Jaxon's with our family hijinks."

No one spoke.

"Derek?" Mr. Drelincourt said.

Derek huffed. "Why me?"

"You've *never* been known to pull a prank, have you?" Rob said.

Derek grinned, white teeth gleaming. "Yeah, well, I certainly wasn't the only one." He sobered again. "But this time I didn't have anything to do with it."

"You sure you packed the books in the first place?" Rob narrowed his eyes at Skip. "You didn't need a little ready cash last time you were at the poker table?"

"Yes, I'm sure, Officer Drelincourt," Skip retorted. "They were in my suitcase, and now they're not."

"Did you have them last night when you arrived?" Faith asked.

"I tell you they were in my suitcase. Right where I packed them."

"But did you see them after you got here?" Faith pressed, trying to ignore the tightening knots in her stomach. "Could someone have taken them out at the airport? Or before you left home?"

"Yeah, well, there's nobody at home anymore but Petie, and he sure didn't take them." Skip shifted in his chair. "I'm telling you they were in my suitcase. They *were*."

"After you got here?" Rob asked. "You saw them?"

Skip shrugged. "No, I didn't take them out and check them. I packed them in the suitcase. I brought the suitcase to my room. I didn't take them out of the suitcase. I expected them to still be in the suitcase. Do you want me to draw you a picture?"

Rob turned to Alice. "Did you unpack your books last night?"

"No. I had them in a separate bag, so nothing would spill on them during the trip. I didn't have any reason to open it before this morning."

"That husband of yours could have taken them out," Lloyd said, peering at her from behind his thick glasses.

"Be nice," Tilly murmured.

"Who's to say he didn't?" Lloyd continued. "If David could get something for them, why wouldn't he? He's never cared about what Alice wanted before, so why should he now?"

Alice gave Faith an apologetic smile. "He's not like that. Lloyd and the others have never really gotten to know Davy, so they don't understand, but he wouldn't have taken the books without telling me. He just wouldn't."

"If he didn't take them," Michelle said, "it's because he knew they'd be worth a lot more sold with the complete set than as individual volumes."

"What about you, Eric?" Rob asked. "You got here with your books, right? Lydia didn't take them?"

Eric sighed and stroked the dozing kitten's head. "Unless you think she stowed away in my baggage or sneaked into my room before I checked in, that's not possible. I had the books when I left home. I carried them up to my room last night. This morning, they're gone."

"They couldn't still be in your luggage somewhere, could they?" Wolfe asked. "Did you check everything?"

"Everything," Eric said in a tone that would have made Eeyore sound like Pollyanna. "I should have known something like this would happen if I planned on things going my way for once."

"It's not like a bunch of hardcover books are going to accidentally slip into the pocket of one of your shirts during the plane ride," Skip said. "We all went through our stuff. The books are gone. What are we going to do about it?"

"The only good thing," Tilly observed, "is that it seems nobody's going to get in or out of the manor for at least another couple of days. If the thief has the books squirreled away somewhere, they'll still be right here."

No one said anything after that. They were obviously as baffled as Faith was herself.

"You're the boss," Derek told Wolfe. "What do we do now?"

Wolfe thought for a moment. "Nothing, I guess."

"What do you mean, nothing?" Skip said, slamming one hand down on the table.

"I mean nothing," Wolfe said calmly. "Nothing until we find out more about what's happened. If you three brought the books to the manor as you claim, then they must still be here somewhere. No one will have an opportunity to smuggle them out anytime soon, so I don't see any reason to panic yet."

Faith glanced from one Drelincourt to another, trying to read each expression, but all she saw was a mixture of anger, fear, confusion, and mistrust. "He's right," she said. "Until the snow clears, the books aren't going anywhere. We just have to find them. Unless you think we should involve the police."

"No, no," Mr. Drelincourt said quickly. "There's no need for that at this point, is there? As you say, the books are here. I wouldn't want to involve the authorities unless it's absolutely necessary."

"Well," Rob said, "I work for the Pasadena PD. I'm a beat cop, not a detective, but I know a little bit about investigations. Maybe I could do some poking around."

"What about those two guys who showed up last night?" Eric asked. "You don't think they might have taken them, do you? They arrived at a weird time."

"Don't be stupid," Skip said. "Two guys off the street get stuck here, and somehow they know we have valuable books in our luggage? I guess they planned the snowstorm too, right?"

Faith wasn't sure Eric's idea should be so readily dismissed. Skip had seemed concerned about them earlier.

Nadine gave Eric a saccharine smile. "Real life doesn't work like one of your bad plots, honey."

Eric sighed and sank down into his chair.

"Well, we have the rest of the books," Faith said. "Nothing can happen to *them*, so why don't we look them over? Then when the other books are found—"

"*If* they're found," Derek said.

"*When* they're found," Faith continued, "we'll have already seen these."

Those who hadn't done so already put on gloves, and then there was the rattle of paper as the books were unwrapped for inspection. Even without the missing volumes, it was an impressive collection. As Faith had been told, the books were all in mint condition, first editions, dust-jacketed, and autographed.

"If these have been read, it couldn't have been more than once or twice," she said. "They're in pristine shape."

"After the first few," Mr. Drelincourt said, "my grandfather always bought two copies. One to read and pass around, and another to have autographed and put away. My father was downright fastidious with them before he died." He gazed around the table at his nieces and nephews. "We've all been taught to treat them with care."

It took some time to go through the books, evaluating them against the descriptions of the ones Faith had sales records for, but eventually it was done.

"It's a beautiful collection," she said. "I'm not sure what all of you would like to do about making an offer to sell. Obviously, if the collection is incomplete, that will impact the price."

Wolfe shook his head. "I'm sorry, but I'm not sure we'd be interested in buying if the other books aren't found. That's something I'd have to seriously consider and discuss with Faith."

"Fabulous," Skip muttered, and Petie leaned against his foot with a soft whine. "Just fabulous."

"We hope that won't be the case," Faith said, glancing at Wolfe. "I'll go ahead and figure an offer based on what we've seen so far and assuming the other books are genuine and in the same condition. After that, you can all get together and decide if you want to accept."

"That seems fair," Mr. Drelincourt said.

John had sat quietly at the table, but now he spoke up. "I don't know."

Everyone turned to him.

"I don't know," he said again, keeping his eyes downcast, "if I'm quite ready to agree to sell."

"Why didn't you say so before we came out here?" Michelle asked, clearly exasperated.

"I just—well, I thought—"

"We were supposed to bring the books for you to look at," Lloyd said. "To *see* if we wanted to sell. We didn't promise anything."

"I realize that," Faith said evenly.

"It's just . . ." John reached down and put one hand on Ahnold's head, his mouth suddenly in a firm line. "I don't know if I want to sell at any price."

Alice touched the dust jacket on *Murder on the Orient Express*. "It's such a nice collection when you see it all together. Mostly all together, I mean. It does seem like it would be a shame if it wasn't in the family anymore. I don't know if Grandpa would have wanted us to sell it."

"He left them to us." Nadine pursed her lips. "He didn't say we couldn't sell them."

"They're not worth nearly as much separately as together," Eric said, staring into the crackling hearth fire. "I guess that was what he wanted us to realize. About the books *and* ourselves. Never mind that Lydia will demand her half of the community property one way or another. Once we're actually divorced."

"I kinda like having them all in the family," Rob said. "We ought to have some sort of connection between us, right?"

Michelle snickered. "Yes, as long as we have the Christies, we'll always be a family."

"That's not what he said," Tilly told her. "And Alice is right—they're very nice all together."

"'Very nice' doesn't exactly keep the wolf away from the door," Skip said, turning toward the library entrance. "Come on, Til. They're just books. If somebody's willing to pay for them—and pay pretty well, I might add—then why not?"

Faith followed his gaze to the door. What was Skip expecting to see? Or whom? Why did Eric seem so unsurprised at losing his part of the collection? And what was Alice afraid of?

"Perhaps," Faith suggested, "we should lock up the books until we figure out what's going on. To keep them safe."

"Not mine," Derek said, stacking his books in front of him on the table. "I can see to them myself, thank you very much."

Nadine gathered up her own books. "Drivel or not, nobody's getting mine either." She looked at Skip. "And they're definitely not going to end up paying anyone's gambling debts."

Skip's face reddened. "I tell you, I had those books with me when I got here. I don't know what happened to them, and I sure didn't take anyone else's."

"Let's not make accusations," Mr. Drelincourt said. "We don't have any evidence yet. I think it's a good idea to lock the books up, as Faith says. But if you don't want to do that, then keep a close eye on your part of the collection until we find the rest of it."

Rob studied each of his relatives. "Maybe the best thing to do is search everybody's room and luggage."

"We can't make that sort of suggestion on behalf of the manor," Wolfe said, "but if everyone agrees and Rob wants to head up the search, being a policeman and all, I think that's a great idea. Does anyone object?"

"What would it hurt?" Tilly asked.

"I don't like it." Derek crossed his arms over his chest. "What is this? The Spanish Inquisition?"

"I don't like it either," Skip said. "It's nobody's business what's in my suitcase. I told you I don't have my books or anyone else's. That ought to be enough."

"You can refuse if you want," Rob said with a casual shrug, "but that makes you suspect number one. Just sayin'."

"No pressure or anything," Michelle purred.

"You can search my room if you want," Lloyd told Rob. "I don't mind."

Nadine sniffed. "I have nothing to hide."

"It wouldn't need to be a deeply involved search, would it?" Faith asked. "After all, if that many books are missing, they're not going to be easy to hide."

Alice bit her lip. "I don't want Lucy to be more upset than she already is. She never did travel well."

"We'll be careful," Rob said.

Alice turned apologetically to Skip and John and then reluctantly looked at Nadine. "I-I think it would be better if you didn't bring the dogs into my room. But it's fine if you search my stuff."

Rob nodded. "Anyone else have comments? Concerns? Skip?"

Skip snorted. "Whatever. Do it if you want to. Just get it over with."

7

"We didn't find anything important in anyone's luggage," Faith said, taking a bite of a delicious seafood crepe.

With the shortage of kitchen staff due to the snowstorm, she and her aunt had both volunteered to help Brooke prepare the noon meal for the guests. Now, at last, the three of them had time for their own lunch in the manor's basement kitchen.

"There were two magazines about muscle cars and a book on card counting in Skip's carry-on bag," Faith told them. "Rob passed over those without comment."

"But no Christie books," Eileen said as she added more vinaigrette to her salad.

"No Christie books," Faith admitted. "Nadine had knitting needles, two skeins of gray yarn, and a stack of essays on Proust to grade. Eric apparently does his first drafts on yellow legal pads, and he had a ton of those in his suitcase, mostly scribbled on. No books. But we were all surprised when Rob pulled a gun out of Derek's duffel bag."

"A gun!" Brooke said.

Faith laughed. "I promise you that's what everyone said when Rob turned it up. But it's an old one, an English Webley from World War I. No bullets, no firing pin. Derek said he'd brought the gun back from overseas, and he thought his uncle might like to have it for his collection. But no books."

"If it was supposed to be a surprise for Mr. Drelincourt, no wonder he didn't want his things searched," Eileen said.

"He seems the type to object just on the principle of the thing," Faith told her, "not because he has anything to hide."

Brooke didn't seem entirely convinced. "Not *just* because he has anything to hide anyway."

"Why him more than anyone else?" Faith asked.

Brooke shrugged. "I have this feeling. He's like some kind of big jungle cat, you know? With gleaming white fangs."

Faith had thought the same thing when she first met him.

Eileen laughed. "Does he have fangs?"

"Of course not." Faith shook her head and took a bite of salad.

"If Diva and Bling were anywhere near him, they'd be all kinds of crazy," Brooke insisted.

"You and your fish," Faith said, crunching down on a piece of crisp radish. "Where are they anyway? I don't think you're going to be home to feed them anytime soon."

"I was afraid the weather would get bad," Brooke said, "so I left them with my neighbor in case I got snowed in. They'll be fine, even if they're not here to be my little fishy radar."

"When did you see Derek?" Faith asked.

"He was poking around near the butler's pantry early today. He said he was interested in how the house is laid out, but he doesn't seem like the architecture aficionado type to me." Brooke wrinkled her nose. "I suppose he could be attractive. Maybe. But he's presumptuous. Diva and Bling would not have approved of the way he was looking at me when we were talking."

Eileen patted her hand. "You'll just have to stop being so darn cute."

Brooke laughed. "I'll make a note of that."

"I'm glad someone is having a good time," Marlene said from the doorway.

Brooke swallowed noisily. Faith felt irrationally guilty.

"Hello, Marlene." Eileen smiled. "We're having a lovely time, in fact. Won't you join us?"

Marlene pulled out a chair and sat down. "Wolfe told me about the missing books. I would have thought you'd be more concerned, Faith."

"I am concerned," Faith said. "But I'm sure Wolfe must have mentioned that, snowed in as we are, those books aren't going anywhere."

"What kind of reputation do you think incidents like this give Castleton Manor?" Marlene retorted. "It makes it appear as if we can't even keep our guests' belongings secure in their own rooms."

"I realize that," Faith said, careful to keep her tone even. "The rooms were searched."

"And that's something else." Marlene shook her head, aghast. "How could you do something like that? It's illegal. If word gets out that we search our guests' rooms—"

"*I* didn't do anything. Rob Drelincourt is a police officer. He did the search, and it was with the consent of each of his family members. Guests are allowed to let family members look in their rooms, aren't they?"

Marlene still seemed displeased. "It's not the sort of reputation we want the manor to have."

Brooke helped herself to more salad. "Well, none of us has the books. We can't search the rooms. What do you want us to do?"

"I don't know. Something. Figure out what's going on. I'm sure Wolfe and the family would rather we didn't involve the police if we can avoid it."

"They're not likely to make it out here in this weather anyway," Eileen said. She popped a cherry tomato into her mouth. "Not for anything less than attempted murder."

"Thank goodness it's just missing books." Faith exhaled heavily. "I don't know who could have taken them or where they could be." She ate another bite, thinking. "I didn't say anything earlier, but Skip came to talk to me before the meeting. He said he wanted to see the library, but he really wanted to know what I knew about our extra guests."

"Mr. Morris and Mr. West," Marlene said, looking as if the shrimp had gone bad.

"I think he must be acquainted with them," Faith said. "Do you know anything about them?"

Marlene sniffed. "They're not our typical clientele. The addresses they gave are in Las Vegas. This Skip person seems like the Vegas type."

"Like organized crime guys?" Brooke asked.

"That's not even funny," Marlene snapped.

"I wasn't trying to be funny."

Faith frowned. "I suppose it's a possibility."

She didn't like that possibility. Not in the least. But Skip had seemed unsettled by them. What had he gotten himself into? Or was he perhaps in on a plot to take the Christie collection? If Skip had debts—especially if he owed the wrong people—maybe he was desperate enough to steal from his own family.

"Is there any way we can search the rooms of Mr. Morris and Mr. West?" Brooke said. "No, I know. Not allowed."

"Maybe I could talk to them," Eileen suggested. "Just casually, you know, to find out a little more about them."

Marlene stood. "Whatever you do, be careful. And if you discover anything that pertains to the thefts, let me know right away." She strode to the kitchen door and then turned. "We've got to figure out what's going on before the snow melts."

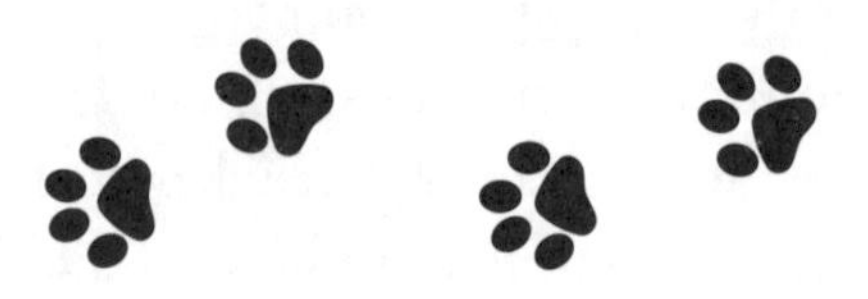

The snow showed no sign of melting. The storm showed no sign of stopping. Faith spent the afternoon in the library working on her detailed bid for the Christie collection, stopping often to mull over the problem of the missing books and even more often to shoo Watson away from Mr. Darcy when Nadine was using some of the reference books.

The Chihuahua certainly didn't like cats, and Watson always made a point of annoying whomever he decided was the biggest ailurophobe in any group. He'd seen Don Quixote when Eric came into the library to look up something in a Barbara Cartland book but evidently didn't find the sleeping kitten adequately interesting. Faith had watched Watson take a daring walk past Ahnold a time or two when John and Skip were playing billiards, then decide he shouldn't press his luck when dealing with German shepherds. Petie had made an attempt to play chase with him, but Watson had put an immediate stop to any such idea with a well-placed swat to the dog's nose.

Lucy was still in hiding, but Watson seemed determined to find her. Several times, Faith had found him wandering down the corridor toward the Drelincourt quarters. Twice she had found him sticking his front paws under Alice's door. Of course, he was always deeply offended by closed doors. Obviously, a cat should be able to go wherever he wanted whenever he wanted. Faith was glad he didn't have opposable thumbs. Then there would be no stopping him.

Fortunately for her, Watson found a cozy spot near the library fireplace and went to sleep for several hours, giving her a chance to finish up the bid for the collection and talk to Wolfe about it.

"I did one for if the missing books were found," she told him, showing him her calculations, "and another for if they aren't."

Wolfe looked it over. "I still don't know if I even want to make a bid if the collection's not complete. What do you think?"

"It would be disappointing if we don't find the missing ones, but the rest of the collection is pretty impressive. It's possible that we could replace the others over time."

"It seems like it wouldn't be the same that way. I'm not sure if we could match the quality of the rest of the collection. And that might be a pretty expensive proposition too, even if we found the right books."

Faith sighed. "I know. Do you want me to tell them the deal's off if the other books aren't found?"

"No."

"So you want me to give them the bid for the incomplete collection?"

"No. Let's see what happens before we tell the Drelincourts anything definitive about what we'll do if the collection isn't complete. I know those books are in the manor somewhere. They'll turn up." Wolfe got up from the table, paced over to the window, and pulled back the heavy curtain as Skip had done earlier in the day. There was only a swirling frenzy of white on the other side of the frosted glass. "Maybe that policeman can do something to help." He didn't turn from the window. "He seems friendly enough."

"He does." Faith kept her voice and her expression professional. "Since the local police are occupied elsewhere, it wouldn't hurt to have him help us find out what's going on."

Wolfe didn't say anything else for a long moment. "Go ahead and make them your offer on the complete set," he said finally. "Contingent, of course, on those missing books being found in excellent condition. It's a good offer under those constraints. Don't say anything about what we might do if the books aren't found. If they ask, just say we'll address that if and when we come to it." He turned back to her. "After the storm is over."

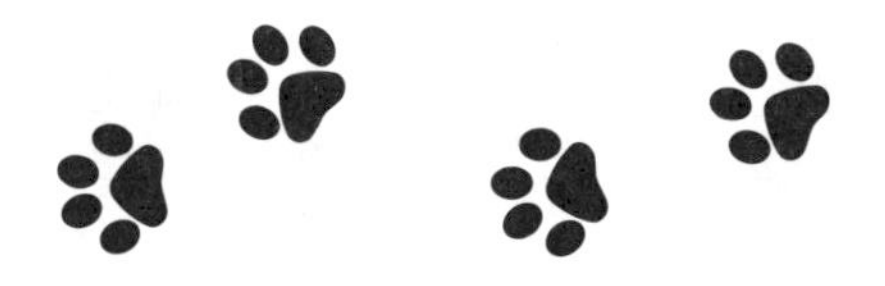

To bulk up Brooke's skeleton crew, Faith and Eileen helped clean up the kitchen that evening. The Drelincourts had been kind enough to invite Faith and her aunt to join them for dinner.

"At least it's only eleven Drelincourts and two mystery men," Eileen said as she scrubbed out a pan that had once been full of zucchini herb casserole, "and not the upcoming Western romance retreat."

"It's nice of you two to pitch in." Brooke put the chicken piccata leftovers into a sealed plastic container and popped it into the freezer. "We might need this if the storm goes on much longer."

"Oh, please," Faith said. "We've been snowed in for less than a day."

"Then I'll probably drop it off to my neighbor as a thank-you for taking care of Diva and Bling."

Eileen grinned. "That cute firefighter who lives across the street, right?"

"I wish. It's for Mrs. Sutton," Brooke said.

"Too bad your cute firefighter isn't with us," Faith told her. "Between him and the policeman, maybe we'd all feel safer."

"Judging by their chat during dinner," Eileen said, giving Brooke a knowing glance, "it seems Faith and the policeman are doing just fine as it is."

Faith rolled her eyes. "Don't be silly. Rob seems like a nice guy, but he's only being friendly. Stop trying to match me up with every eligible man who comes to the manor." She made her expression stern. "Or lives in it."

Brooke and Eileen laughed.

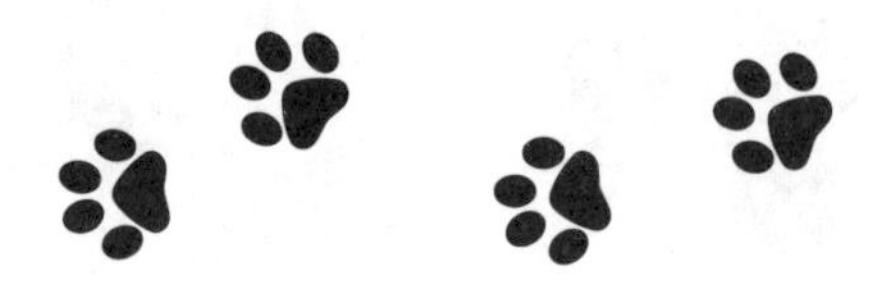

Faith didn't even try to get back to the cottage that night. Marlene gave her the room next to Eileen's, and she quickly made herself at home. When she was about to get ready for bed, she went out into the corridor to see if she could find Watson. She didn't have much hope of spotting him in such a big place, especially if he didn't want to be found, but she could at least take a turn around the floor.

It was quiet in the hallway. The guests were probably in their rooms. Maybe some of them were still down in the common areas, playing cards or billiards or socializing, but Faith didn't see anyone, and she was too tired to go downstairs and see who was still up.

As she was walking toward the Drelincourt end of the floor, she heard a door being opened behind her. She turned and walked toward it. There was no one in the part of the hall she could see, but there were more rooms around the corner. Morris and West were the only ones staying in that section, and she hoped Watson hadn't figured out some way to bother them.

She peeked around the corner and was startled to see Laura emerging from one of the rooms. West's? Morris's? Faith wasn't sure. Laura didn't have her housekeeping cart with her, but why would she be cleaning rooms at this time of night anyway?

Laura carried a fluffy, white towel. She cast a furtive glance around, shut the door behind her, and darted off, most likely toward the stairs.

Faith scanned the hallway, saw no sign of Watson, and then walked back the way she had come and over toward the Drelincourt rooms.

She found Watson camped outside Alice's door and had to carry him, protesting, into their temporary quarters.

"Lucy will come out if and when she's ready," Faith told him as she dumped him on the luxurious king-size bed. "And if she does come out, she's not going to want you stalking her."

Watson merely stretched out on the coverlet.

"And leave Mr. Darcy alone." She scratched his back just above his stubby tail. "Do you hear me, Rumpy?"

With a huff, Watson rolled over, refusing to look at her any longer.

"Fine." Faith went into the bathroom to get ready for bed. She was too tired to worry about what Watson had been up to. Or Laura for that matter. There was time enough to worry about that tomorrow after she had a good night's sleep.

The ringing of her cell phone next to the bed woke Faith from a deep sleep. The red digital readout from the alarm clock on the nightstand read 2:27.

"Hello?" Her voice was thick with sleep, so she cleared her throat and tried again. "Hello?"

"We have a problem," Marlene said.

"What's wrong?" Faith fumbled for the light and switched it on.

Watson blinked from the pillow beside her, looking as if he had also been sound asleep.

"One of the Drelincourts, the one with the German shepherd."

"John?" Faith asked. "Is something wrong with him?"

"It's the dog. The one with the ridiculous name. You know more about this sort of thing than I do. Maybe you can tell if it's serious or not."

"I'm not sure if I know any more about dogs than you do, but I'll come. Give me a minute to put something on. Which room is he in?"

"Brontë," Marlene said. "We'll be waiting for you."

When Faith reached the Brontë Suite, she found Marlene standing at the door.

They went in, and Marlene shut the door behind them.

John was sitting on the bed, his lean face lined with worry. Ahnold lay unmoving beside him with his heavy head in John's lap.

"He won't wake up." John lifted one broad paw and then let it fall. "I can't get him to wake up."

8

"Is he breathing?" Faith hurried to the bed and put one hand on the dog's side. She was relieved to feel it move, to feel the heart thudding slow and steady. "He seems all right, just asleep."

"But why won't he wake up?" John asked.

"I don't know," Faith told him, imagining how terrified she would feel if Watson was lying there unresponsive. "Marlene, we need to call Midge right away."

"Midge?" John asked, putting his arm around the limp body of his dog. "Who's Midge? He needs a vet."

"Midge Foster is the local vet," Faith said soothingly, "and she's excellent at her job. She'll be able to tell us what's going on."

Marlene shook her head. "She's not going to be able to do anything in this weather."

"We can call her. That won't hurt anything." Faith went to the phone by the bed and dialed Midge's number. Then she remembered what Marlene had said about the landlines being down and felt silly. She pulled her cell phone from her pocket and punched in Midge's number again. "Midge, hi. It's Faith. I'm so sorry to bother you in the middle of the night."

"What's the matter?" Midge's Alabama accent was more pronounced than usual. "Is Watson all right?"

"He's fine. Listen, I'm staying at the manor overnight because of the storm, and one of the guests has a German shepherd that's having some problems. I thought maybe you could tell us what to do."

"Sure." Midge's husband murmured something in the

background, and she told him to wait a minute. "Sorry, Faith. Now tell me what's going on."

"I really don't know. He seems to be fine, but he won't wake up."

"He's breathing all right? Heart beating?"

"Yes," Faith said. "It seems a little slow to me but normal. Like he's just in a deep sleep."

"Has anything like this happened before?"

Faith relayed the question.

John shook his head. "He's always been healthy."

Faith told Midge what John said, then added, "Maybe you'd better talk directly to him."

John took the phone, and with each answer he gave Midge, he appeared more upset. "No, he doesn't take any medications . . . I didn't give him anything unusual to eat . . . He didn't get into anything he shouldn't have, as far as I know." He squeezed Ahnold closer to him, making the dog's head loll backward. "Please, Doctor, you have to do something for him. Please."

Faith was glad Watson was in her room, safe and sound. She glanced at Marlene, and the assistant manager immediately turned away.

"Okay," John said after a moment. "Yes. Got it. Thank you." He handed the phone back to Faith, then leaned down to kiss the top of Ahnold's head, whispering something against his bristly fur.

"What are we supposed to do?" Marlene asked him.

"Just hang on," John said. "She's coming."

"What?" Faith went to the window. The snow wasn't falling as heavily now, but it covered everything in deep, soft drifts. "There's no way she can get here."

"She says she can," John said, his attention still on Ahnold. "She said her husband has a truck with tire chains and four-wheel drive."

That was just like Midge, ready to do anything to help a sick animal, even at the risk of her own safety. At least it wasn't that far from her house to the manor.

"I assume there's nothing else I can do at this point," Marlene said, glancing at the bedside clock. "But let me know if you need anything."

John nodded, looking faintly miserable.

"Do you want me to wait with you?" Faith asked.

Again he nodded.

"I'll send Midge up when she gets here," Marlene said and shut the door behind her.

Faith sat on the bed, stroking the dog's tawny muzzle. "Have you had him a long time?"

"Nearly ten years," John said with a tight smile. "Since before I was married." His smile turned a little bittersweet. "Almost didn't get married. Jen said I'd have to get rid of him or we were through. She didn't want to live with a 'big fleabag.'" John stroked the dog's black ears. "You never had fleas, did you, boy?"

"She must have changed her mind."

"I think I surprised her when I said I couldn't get rid of him. I guess I hadn't told her no about much of anything before that." John shrugged. "Or since. We've got three kids now and her mother living with us, but Ahnold's mine." He hugged the limp dog closer. "He listens to me."

"We all need someone like that," she said encouragingly. "I don't think I ever heard what you do for a living."

"Me? I'm an administrative assistant. It's a nice title, but sometimes I feel like a glorified waiter or a butler or something. Everybody telling me what to do and when. Get this, bring me that, and take care of this." He sighed. "Just like at home."

Faith looked at him sympathetically, not knowing what else to say.

John finally gave her a weak smile. "I guess if the job was fun, I'd have to pay them, right?"

"I guess so." It would probably make him more depressed if she told him how much she loved her own job. Instead she stroked Ahnold's nose again. "Did he act strange earlier tonight? Sick?"

John shook his head. "He was fine when I went to dinner. When I got back, he was asleep on the bed just like that. I didn't think anything of it. I got into bed next to him and went to sleep. When I woke up a little while ago, I pulled him over close to me. Usually, that wakes him up, but this time he didn't stir." The anxious lines came back into his face. "No matter what I did, he didn't move."

"Why didn't you take him down to dinner?"

"I thought he could stay up here and make sure nobody—" John sat up straight. "The books!" He slid the dog's head off his lap and jumped up.

Faith went with him to the closet, watching as he flung open the door and dragged out a carry-on bag.

"No," John said, hefting it as if testing its weight before tossing it onto the bed.

The bag had two zipper pulls. He fumbled with it for a minute, tugging one way and then the other before it opened wide enough for Faith to see inside.

"No. No, no, no!" He rummaged around in the bag, feeling through the clothes, shoving aside a smaller bag that must have contained toiletries and other sundries. There wasn't anything else to find.

The books were gone.

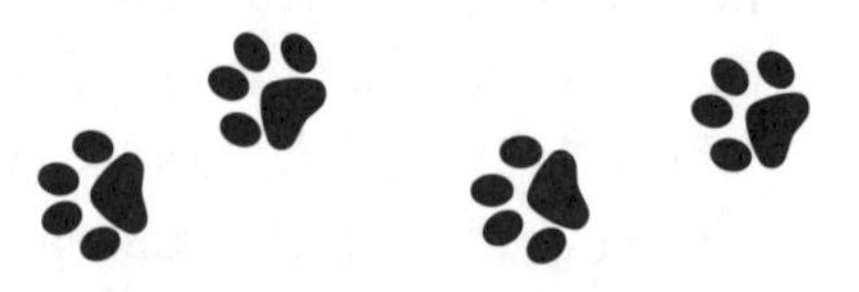

It was a long while before Midge, cold and wet with snow, made it up to John's room. By then they at least had a theory about what was wrong with Ahnold.

"I think someone must have drugged him," Faith told Midge. "To be able to get to John's books."

Midge lifted the dog's right eyelid and shone a light into the pupil. Then she did the same with the left. "It's looking that way."

John clenched his jaw. "That's a nasty thing to do."

A few minutes later, Midge finished her examination and started repacking her bag. "I think you're right about the drugging. I can't find anything actually wrong with him. He's not in distress, and he doesn't seem to be getting any worse. I expect he'll sleep it off and be fine in another few hours." She patted John's arm. "I don't think you need to worry about him, but I'll be back in the morning to check on him."

John nodded and thanked her.

Faith and Midge went to Faith's room. Watson looked up sleepily when the door opened and then, seeing who Faith had brought with her, was suddenly alert. Of course, it wouldn't do to go straight to Midge. He had to stretch and preen and, once more, groom his left front paw. Then he had to stretch again and make his circuitous and nonchalant way over to where Midge was standing. She owned the Happy Tails bakery where Faith bought Watson's tunaroons. He wasn't about to forget her.

"Yes, I remember you," Midge said, giggling as he rubbed his face against her shin. "And I brought you something." She dug around in her bag and presented him with a fresh treat.

While he was occupied, she and Faith sat down at the table in front of the room's curtained window.

"Did you have much trouble getting over here?" Faith asked.

"It's not just snow out there now. There's ice for extra fun." Midge winced. "I slid into a tree out front, and I couldn't get the truck moving again. Peter's not going to be happy about that."

"Uh-oh. I'm surprised he didn't insist on coming with you."

"He wanted to. Well, actually, he didn't want me to come at all. Somebody had to stay with Atticus, and I didn't want to risk Peter getting stuck with me." Atticus was Midge's Chihuahua, and she doted on the tiny dog.

"There's another Chihuahua staying here right now," Faith told her. "Mr. Darcy."

Midge looked over at Watson. "And you devil him just as bad as you do Atticus, don't you?"

"He seems more interested in the tabby that's visiting. But Lucy's a recluse so far and doesn't want to play."

"Poor little girl," Midge said. "Some animals don't enjoy seeing new places. Cats especially."

"Well, I'm sorry you had to come out and wreck Peter's truck for something that wasn't serious."

Midge shook her head. "I don't think the truck's much hurt. It's not that new anyway. And I would have hated staying home and then finding out the shepherd was in real trouble. That poor man loves him."

Faith nodded. "What do you think they gave him?"

"I don't know without testing. It'll probably be out of his system well before the ice melts."

"It's a shame we won't be able to find out what was used on him."

"But what's going on?" Midge asked. "What's this about stolen books?"

Faith quickly filled her in on what had happened since the Drelincourts' arrival. "But maybe between you, me, Brooke, and Aunt Eileen, we can find out who's behind the thefts."

"Eileen's here? I figured Brooke might have gotten snowed in but not Eileen."

Faith laughed softly. "You know her. She was determined not to let a little snow keep her from seeing those Christie first editions, but she ended up stuck here with us. I'm glad, though. I don't like the idea of her driving home in this mess."

"It should be interesting for the four of us anyway. The Candle House Book Club gets to solve a real mystery, not just a fictional one." Midge yawned, belatedly putting one hand over her mouth. "Sorry. I think sleep is catching up with me. Marlene said I could have the room next door, so I guess I'll go call Peter and then turn in."

Watson gave an ingratiating little purr and sauntered over to Midge, his treat now just a pleasant memory.

"Sweet dreams," Midge said, leaning down to stroke his head. "No more treats for tonight."

He narrowed his eyes and, head held high, walked back to the bed and stretched out again.

Faith woke a little before eight in the morning and quickly showered and dressed.

Watson watched her from near the door to the hallway, apparently waiting for his chance to snoop around the rest of the manor.

"All right, all right." She opened the door, and he shot out. Only then did she realize that he was carrying Ahnold's stuffed pig. How in the world had he gotten it away from the German shepherd and smuggled it into her room?

"Watson, bring that back," she said, keeping her voice low. "Watson."

As always, he pretended he didn't hear her.

"The dog will eat you alive if you don't return his toy," she told him. "And if Lucy's out there, she won't think you're all that suave, running around like a kitten."

Watson didn't turn, but he slowed to a disinterested walk, nose in the air, pig held high.

"He's cute."

Faith turned to see Laura pushing a laundry cart from the other end of the floor. Laura. With everything that had happened, Faith had forgotten about her being in Morris's or West's room. She had to find out what was going on.

Laura hurried up to her, looking around to make sure they were unobserved. "Was that German shepherd really poisoned?"

"How did you hear about that? No, he wasn't poisoned. Probably drugged, but Midge says he should be fine. I'm on my way to check on him."

"That's good to know." Laura tucked a wispy strand of hair behind her ear. "One of the other girls told me Dr. Foster came in last night because of the dog. I don't know how she managed. It's all ice out there now."

"I don't think her husband's going to be happy about that part, but I'm sure he's glad she's safe here." Faith lowered her voice. "I saw you coming out of Mr. Morris's room last night. Or was it Mr. West's? What's going on?"

"I was just—" Laura twined her thin, white fingers together. "I might have done something I shouldn't have."

"What do you mean?"

"While Mr. Morris and Mr. West were in the billiard room playing cards, I took my passkey and—"

"Laura." Faith forced an even tone. "Don't tell me you searched their rooms."

Laura bit her lip and nodded rapidly.

"I hope Marlene didn't see you."

"No, of course not. I made sure she was still in the office doing some paperwork. I wasn't in either room long." Laura swallowed hard. "I was so scared every second I was in there. I heard what Ms. Russell said about the two of them, coming from Las Vegas and everything. I didn't want them to catch me."

"You didn't disturb anything, I hope."

"No, I hardly touched anything. I looked really quick in their drawers and closets and suitcases. Just enough to tell if there were any books. But one of the other girls had cleaned in there that morning. If I got caught I was going to say someone had called asking for an extra towel. That's why I was carrying one."

"I don't know who those two men are or who they might work for, but if they're the type of guys we think they might be, what you did was highly dangerous. Not to mention illegal."

"I'm sorry," Laura said, ducking her head. "I was only trying to help."

"It's all right," Faith said, her expression softening. "I know you were. I got the 'no illegal searches' lecture from Marlene yesterday. I don't want either of us to get into trouble."

Laura looked up at her, eyes earnest. "You've been so nice to me, and I didn't want something to ruin your big chance to buy the books and impress Mr. Jaxon."

"I appreciate that, but please be more careful. And don't worry. We'll figure it out."

"I guess we'll have a lot of time to talk about it," Laura said. "I don't think you'll be able to get back to your cottage tonight."

"Don't tell me it's gotten even worse overnight."

"The snow's getting deeper, and you can't see more than a foot or two from the window." Laura smiled a little. "Good thing you brought Watson with you. I'm sure you'd be pretty worried about him."

Faith laughed. "Maybe if I can keep him from trying to tease Mr. Darcy, he can help us discover what happened to the missing books. Did you hear that more books were taken?"

"No. Really?"

"John Drelincourt's. He's the one who has the German shepherd."

"That's awful, and after he was already worried about his dog. It's mean for someone to do that." Laura glanced over her shoulder and lowered her voice. "It's getting a little freaky around here."

"Just remember it's our job as professionals to keep confidential things confidential. No gossiping with the other girls or talking about what's going on with the guests, especially about the thefts and what happened to the dog." Faith gave the younger woman a warning look. "Of course, I want you to keep your eyes and ears open for anything unusual, but be careful. No more snooping around by yourself."

Laura nodded and left with her cart.

Faith walked down the corridor to the Brontë Suite and knocked. She was happy to hear a hearty bark from inside.

John opened the door. "Oh, hi." He stepped back. "As you can see, Ahnold's doing fine. The vet was in here about half an hour ago to check on him. She says whatever drug he was given doesn't seem to have any permanent effects."

Inside the door, the dog was lying at John's feet, bright-eyed and alert, nothing like he had been a few hours before.

Faith leaned down to pat his head, but before she could say anything, the door to the room at their left flew open and Nadine burst out with Mr. Darcy clutched against her, two spots of angry red in her ghost-pale cheeks.

"Are you all right?" John asked her. "Come sit down."

"They're gone," Nadine fumed, pushing past Faith in the doorway and dropping into a chair. "All my books have been stolen."

9

"Gone," Nadine repeated as the Drelincourts whose suites were nearby peered out of their doors and then came over to John's room. A few of the others, already walking down the hall, heard the commotion and walked in as well.

"It's outrageous!" Nadine said, her voice quivering. "I was about to go down to breakfast, but I thought I should make sure my books were all right first. So I opened the suitcase I had packed them in, and they were gone. I can't believe it. I can't believe this has happened to four of us now."

"Five," John said. "Mine were taken too. Whoever did it gave Ahnold something to put him out while he stole the books."

Nadine clutched her Chihuahua closer and stared at Faith. "What kind of place is this? I can't even—"

"Just hold on." Mr. Drelincourt made his way around Michelle and Lloyd and went to Nadine. "Faith doesn't know any more about the missing books than we do. John, what's this about you and Ahnold?"

Before John could reply, Nadine gripped her uncle's arm and said, "I don't feel safe. And Mr. Darcy, poor baby, what if something happened to him? He's quite delicate. Not a big lump like John's dog."

Mr. Drelincourt patted her hand. "You're both all right, aren't you? No need for anyone to panic. Why don't we go down to breakfast, and Nadine and John can tell us what's happened. No need to repeat it ten times. Are we all here? Who are we missing?" He looked out into the hallway.

"Alice isn't up yet," Tilly said. "Her room's the farthest one on the other side of the floor. She probably didn't hear anything."

"She's just late again," Skip said. "I'll go get her, and we'll meet you in the breakfast room." He loped off toward the far corridor.

"I'm not leaving my books in my room. Not after this." Lloyd stared down the hallway after Skip, a perplexed little pucker between his tufted red brows. "Until I find a good hiding place, I'm keeping my books with me."

"I think I'll do the same," Michelle said, "but doesn't Skip have to go past your rooms, Derek? Rob?"

"Now I didn't say anything about Skip," Lloyd protested. "But I guess it wouldn't hurt to go check on our books, right, Rob?"

"You didn't say anything," Derek said, "but you made it pretty clear what you were thinking. Well, I thought it way before you did, and I'm not going to be caught off guard by anyone." His gaze was cool and calculating. "No matter who the thief is."

All the cousins appeared uncomfortable, and their uncle was obviously distressed.

Faith thought she knew how Mr. Drelincourt must be feeling. Surely none of the cousins was stealing from the others. And yet, if they weren't, that meant someone on the Castleton Manor staff was. After all, who else knew about the books, much less their worth?

Mr. Drelincourt took a deep breath, gave Tilly a comforting smile, and turned to Faith. "Would you join us for breakfast?"

"I'd like that, but my aunt—"

"She could eat with us again too, couldn't she, Uncle Max?" Rob's smile was charming. "It'd be a shame for us to miss out on such good company."

"Of course," Mr. Drelincourt said, giving Faith his own charming smile. "We would be pleased to have you both join us."

Faith knew Eileen would love to find out more about this little mystery and meet the major players. *Or major suspects?* "I'll ask her. I'm sure she'll be delighted."

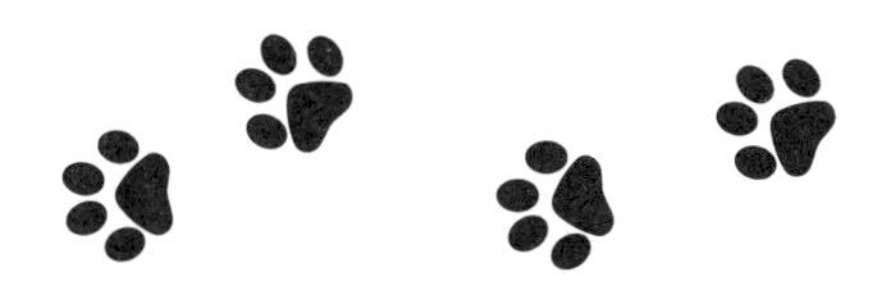

Skip and Alice were already in the breakfast room by the time everyone else arrived. Despite the lack of kitchen help and waitstaff, Brooke had set out a lovely buffet featuring one of Faith's favorites—baked eggs with cheese, spinach, and Canadian bacon. As Faith had expected, Eileen was more than eager to hear about the latest thefts.

"I was in the bathtub, running the water," Nadine said once everyone was settled at the table, "and I thought I heard someone knock." She fed her Chihuahua a piece of bacon. "I thought it was the maid, but I had Mr. Darcy with me in the bathroom, so I didn't worry about him getting out or anything. I didn't think anything of it."

"You didn't think it was unusual for housekeeping to come in while you were in the room?" Faith asked.

"Well, I'm almost sure I heard a knock. And I didn't answer, so I assumed whoever it was thought I was out of the room and came to clean. She must have realized I was in the bathtub, because she left. It didn't strike me as strange at the time, but now I'm sure whoever it was must have taken my books." Nadine smirked. "Not that Christie's writing can be classified as actual literature, but the books themselves are valuable. It's beyond outrageous that someone had the temerity to steal them while I was practically in the room."

Rob glanced at Faith and forked up more eggs. "I'm keeping mine with me from now on." He patted the lumpy canvas bag that lay on the table beside him. The manor provided those bags for guest laundry.

Lloyd and Tilly had their own books, still wrapped, stacked next to their plates. Michelle had a small wheeled carry-on propped against the leg of her chair. Derek had brought nothing to the table except an evidently hearty appetite.

"I'd like to see you write something as good," Lloyd said, his face reddening. "You teach your students how to read books critically, but that's not the same as writing them."

"Those who can't, teach," Michelle added. "By the way, how *is* your novel coming along, Nadine dear?"

Nadine's eyes flashed, but her cool smile did not alter. "It's just experimental. Not meant for publication." She glanced at Eric, who was letting little Don Quixote lick the butter from his toast. "Commercial writers have to make so many compromises in quality. I wouldn't want to write under those constraints."

Eileen gave Faith a look. Clearly, she wanted to know what was between Nadine and Michelle, but Faith could only return a subtle shrug.

"You didn't hear a voice or anything when someone came into your room?" Faith asked, hoping to deflect another argument between the sisters.

"No," Nadine said. "Just a tap on the door and then the door opening and closing. That was all."

"How long between the opening and closing?"

Nadine thought for a moment, letting Mr. Darcy sneak another bite of her bacon. "Maybe thirty seconds," she said finally. "Not more than a minute."

"Everybody else who had their books taken had them packed

in their luggage," Tilly said. "Is that where yours were?"

"I had them under the foot of my mattress," Nadine admitted, looking a little foolish. "I thought they'd be all right there when I was asleep."

"You should have taken them into the bathroom with you," Rob said.

Nadine rolled her eyes and sipped her breakfast tea.

"Did Mr. Darcy bark?" Faith asked, watching the Chihuahua help himself to a bite of Nadine's eggs. "I mean, when you heard the knock."

"Yes, he did. I think."

"He always barks," Lloyd said, and Mr. Darcy obliged by yipping twice. "It doesn't mean he did or didn't know the person who came in."

Skip went to the buffet table and poured another cup of coffee, wincing as he took the first gulp.

"Hot enough for you?" Derek asked.

"Peachy." Skip glanced at the door as he reclaimed his seat. "I was wondering about those two guys who came in off the road the night we got here. What have they been doing lately? Anybody seen them around?"

"I saw them in the game room last night," Alice said, "but I was just there for a minute. I don't know how long they stayed."

"What were they doing?" Skip asked.

"Playing cards."

"Poker, I suppose."

Alice shrugged. "I don't know. The big guy said hello. He was very polite. I said hello, took some cards, and went back to my room. That was it."

"Cards?" Derek said. "You haven't taken up gambling, have you, little sister?"

"Don't be silly. I wanted to play solitaire. I got tired of the book I was reading."

"I saw those two men in the hall near our rooms," Tilly said. "The big guy, the friendly one, asked if I knew where the library was. I don't know how he wouldn't know that."

"By whose room exactly?" Skip asked, sitting up straighter. "Where was the guy?"

"I nearly ran into him when I was coming out of my room," Tilly said. "I don't know why he would have come that way. There's nothing but my room and Uncle Max's at that end."

Skip drank some more coffee while Petie propped his furry chin on his master's foot, seeming perplexed.

Faith didn't say anything, but she remembered that Skip's room was near there, right around the corner from Tilly's. Marlene had also seen the heavyset man, Morris, in that area. Was Skip the reason?

John stroked the brindled fur at the back of his German shepherd's head. "Nobody saw them by our rooms last night, right? I mean, maybe before dinner?"

"Ahnold would have barked at a stranger, wouldn't he?" Mr. Drelincourt asked John.

"I'm sure he would, but he didn't do anything unusual while I was getting ready for dinner."

"Maybe someone pushed something under the door," Eric suggested. "If Ahnold ate it, whoever it was wouldn't have had to go into the room."

Derek chuckled. "Sounds like something out of one of your books. Only the victim would have been a reformed party boy who had been targeted by a corrupt politician and who had just lost his one true love through a tragic misunderstanding."

"Derek," Tilly scolded, "why do you have to be like that?"

"Just a little humor, Til." Derek spread one hand over his heart and made a slight bow from where he sat. "No offense, Eric."

The Drelincourts squabbled through the rest of breakfast, snatching up and discarding accusations like paper napkins. Mr. Drelincourt tried his best to keep them reasonably civil, but he was clearly worn-out. The way Tilly looked after him, Faith couldn't help wondering if the old gentleman was dealing with some chronic health issue. She couldn't decide whether he actually appeared ill, but he did seem tired.

Eileen gave Faith a look that said she was glad she didn't have to deal with this family every day.

The family finally decided there was nothing more to do than keep their eyes open for the missing books and take care of the ones they still had.

Breakfast over, they wandered off in groups of twos and threes, some to play billiards or cards, some to read or otherwise amuse themselves without the assistance of the Internet.

"And those are the Drelincourts," Faith said once she and Eileen were alone.

"They're probably fine taken one at a time." Eileen laughed. "Well, most of them. There has to be some history between Michelle and Nadine, don't you think?"

"I very much think, though I'm not sure it has anything to do with the missing books. I wonder—"

"We have another serious problem." Marlene entered the breakfast room and shut the door. "I understand more of the Christie books are missing."

Faith nodded. "John's were taken last night. Nadine's were probably stolen sometime this morning."

"Those are the ones I'm really concerned about." Marlene glanced at Eileen. "Would you excuse us for a moment?"

"You might want to let her hear what's going on," Faith said, putting one hand on her aunt's arm to keep her from getting up. "The more people we have trying to solve this problem, the better."

"Fine." Marlene sat at the table across from Faith. "Nadine wants to know which one of our staff members was in her room and why we haven't done anything about it."

Faith stared. "You don't really think it was someone who works at the manor, do you? Not many of them are even here because of the weather, and the ones who are have been working here for a long time. Who would you suspect?"

"You're right about the staff," Marlene answered. "But I have to check this out."

"Who was cleaning that section today?"

"That's the problem. It was supposed to be Jennifer, but she said Laura told her she finished her rooms early and volunteered to help her out today." Marlene pursed her lips. "Volunteered."

"I'm sure she only meant to be helpful. You're not saying you think Laura had something to do with the thefts, are you?"

"I'm saying I have to check it out. We have a guest with a complaint," Marlene said. "Not just a complaint but an accusation. We have to take it seriously."

"True," Faith admitted. "But I'm sure Laura would never steal anything."

Marlene's mouth tightened. "I've learned not to be too sure what someone wouldn't do, given the right motivation. I've sent for Laura to join us. We'll find out what she does or doesn't know."

There was a hesitant tap at the door, and Laura appeared. "You wanted to see me, Ms. Russell?" She seemed puzzled to see Faith and Eileen at the table.

"Yes." Marlene pulled out a chair for her. "Please sit down."

Laura did as she was told, her eyes enormous as she glanced from Marlene to Faith and back to Marlene again. "Did I do something wrong?"

Marlene looked at her coldly. "That's what we want to know."

10

Laura licked her lips. "I don't know what you mean. What did I do?"

Faith and Eileen looked at each other. Marlene never bothered with being diplomatic.

"Laura," Faith said, keeping her voice even, "remember when I talked to you this morning? When I was going to John Drelincourt's room to check on his dog?"

Laura nodded.

"You were coming from the other end of the hall with a laundry cart."

Again Laura nodded. "I was helping Jennifer since we're so shorthanded. But I thought I shouldn't go back into Mr. Morris's room or Mr. West's after—" There was a flash of panic in her eyes as she glanced at Faith, and then she steadied herself.

Faith was thankful Laura hadn't blurted out that she had been snooping in their rooms.

"Well, I mean, after what I heard about them," Laura continued, "so I told her I'd do the Drelincourt rooms, at least the ones on that side."

"Did you go into Nadine's room?" Marlene asked. "She's next door to John, who's in the Brontë Suite."

"No. I was going to finish that side after lunch."

"Which rooms did you go into?" Faith asked.

"None of them. Not right then. I was waiting for the guests to go to breakfast." Laura winced, seeing Marlene's icy expression. "Is something wrong?"

"If you hadn't cleaned any rooms," Marlene said, "then what were you doing with that cart?"

Laura's mouth opened, but no sound came out. Then she swallowed and tried again. "I was . . . going to the storage room. It's right around the corner from that section." She bit her lower lip, looking pleadingly at Faith.

"Why were you going to the storage room?" Marlene pressed.

"S-soap. I ran out of guest soaps, so I went to get more. From the storage room."

Marlene pursed her lips. "I see."

Clearly she didn't, and Faith couldn't ignore the nagging feeling in the back of her own mind. Laura was terrified of Marlene, afraid of being fired at the slightest misstep, but did that completely explain her nervousness now? Who would have a better opportunity to get in and out of the guests' rooms without being seen? Or having been seen, who would have a more plausible and innocent excuse?

Surely Laura wouldn't do something so foolish, so detrimental to her plans for bettering her life. But she wanted so badly to finish her degree, to improve herself, to make a future that didn't include endless bed making and bathroom cleaning. Did she want it badly enough to steal for it?

"Is something wrong?" Laura asked again, appearing as if she were fighting tears. "Is this about those books?"

There was a sudden glint in Marlene's eyes. "Why do you ask that?"

"Because I heard more were missing." Now tears did fill Laura's eyes. "You don't think I have them, do you? Please, Ms. Russell, I promise you I'd never do anything like that. I need this job. I wouldn't do something that would get me in trouble. I swear I never took anything."

Marlene held out her hand. "I think you'd better give me your passkey."

"Ms. Russell, please—"

Marlene still held out her hand. "For now I don't want you going into any of the guest rooms without one of the other housekeepers accompanying you."

Ducking her head, Laura fished in her pocket and brought out her passkey. For a moment she hesitated, and then she handed it over.

"Thank you." Marlene put the key in her own pocket. "Now at least the Drelincourts won't think we have done nothing about the situation."

Her face reddening, Laura made no protest.

"Maybe it would be a good idea if none of the staff members go into any of the Drelincourt rooms alone," Faith said, feeling a twinge of guilt. "There's no reason the housekeepers couldn't work in pairs, is there?"

"It seems like a good way to protect the manor from any more guest complaints," Eileen said, giving Laura a sympathetic smile. "And protect the housekeepers. I don't know why you'd want to upset any of your employees with unfounded accusations."

"I haven't accused anyone of anything." Marlene glared at Laura. "Yet."

Laura sniffed and blinked hard. "Did Ms. Drelincourt say I stole her books?"

"No," Marlene admitted. "She just heard someone come in while she was in the bathtub and assumed it was one of the housekeepers. But if you were the only one responsible for that area this morning, then it's only natural—"

"But that could have been anybody," Laura said. "You believe me, don't you, Faith?"

Faith wanted to leap to Laura's defense, but then she remembered her mentioning that she had been in the Brontë Suite, John's room, before the meeting with the Drelincourts yesterday morning. Before anyone knew any books were missing. Laura had claimed she was just looking at the condition of the roads. It had the best view, Faith had to admit. *But still . . .*

"I don't want you to worry," Faith said, her voice not as reassuring as she wished it could be. "Nobody is going to be accused of anything without proof."

Laura's chin quivered, but she nodded. "What do you want me to do, Ms. Russell? I can't go home."

"No," Marlene said, "and I wouldn't expect you to. Go about your usual duties, but none of the staff will work alone until this matter is settled. I don't need to tell you what would happen if I find out you're not telling me the truth."

"No ma'am." At that, Laura left the room, shutting the door soundlessly behind her.

"Well, you've terrorized her," Eileen said sharply.

Marlene frowned. "I had to find out what she knew. What did you want me to do?"

"You could have just asked her what she knew without making accusations." Faith exhaled heavily. "I guess we can't rule her out, but we don't have any real evidence against her either."

"Means, motive, and opportunity," Marlene snapped. "Isn't that what you need for a suspect? She had all three."

"So did a lot of other people," Faith said. "What about your favorite guests? Mr. Morris and Mr. West."

"I guess there is that possibility," Marlene admitted.

"You know they've been seen wandering around in the Drelincourt end of the floor, and that's after you told them to make themselves scarce."

"I do wonder about them," Marlene said. "What's your theory?"

"I still think deliberately getting stuck in a snowstorm so you can steal some valuables at a posh retreat is a pretty stupid plan, but now I'm wondering if their being here is such a coincidence after all. I'm almost positive Skip knows them. Or knows about them from somewhere."

"Vegas," Eileen said decidedly. "That's where the mobsters hang out, don't they?"

"You'd know more about that than I do," Faith said, smiling. "I'm sure you come across characters like that all the time in your mystery books."

Marlene stood, her expression a clear indication that she was in no mood for frivolity. "I'll be glad when this storm is over and the police finally have time for nonemergency issues."

"The worst thing we could do is wait till the storm is over before we do something," Faith said. "At this point we know the books and the thief have to be here somewhere. Once the roads are clear, they are all likely to slip out of our hands."

"Along with Castleton Manor's reputation." Marlene squared her shoulders. "I suppose I have to let Wolfe know that more of the books have been taken. That is, if Nadine Drelincourt hasn't stormed up to the third floor to tell him herself."

Faith flinched.

"Keep your eyes open, and let me know about anything you find." Marlene opened the door just as Brooke and Midge were about to knock.

"The rest of your book club is here," Marlene announced as she stalked off.

"We heard more of the books were stolen," Midge said, sitting across the table from Faith. "Any ideas?"

Brooke shut the door and joined them. "This is much more

exciting than staying home. Even if Diva and Bling can't be here."

"I don't like leaving Atticus either," Midge said, and then she grinned. "But he and Peter can use some bonding time anyway. So what happened with this latest batch of books?"

Faith told her and Brooke everything she knew about what had happened. "I don't like to think that Laura might have had anything to do with it. She doesn't seem like the type. But like Marlene said, she had means, motive, and opportunity."

"I'm with you. I can't see Laura doing anything like this, though it does seem pretty typical of Marlene to scare her out of her wits just for fun." Brooke tapped her fingers on the table. "I think it's Derek Drelincourt. He looks like he's up to something."

"You know," Faith said, "there is something a bit odd there. Only Tilly, Lloyd, Rob, Derek, and Michelle still have their first editions. They're keeping their books with them all the time now for safekeeping. But not Derek."

"Interesting," Midge said. "Did he say why?"

Faith shrugged. "I imagine he's got them tucked away somewhere safe. He didn't say anything about it except that he wasn't going to be caught off guard."

"Either that or he's got his own books and all the rest of them tucked away somewhere safe," Brooke said. "Diva and Bling would never trust him."

"My money's on the two mobsters," Eileen said, her eyes bright. "And I wouldn't be surprised if Skip Drelincourt owes them a lot of money. Probably gambling debts their boss sent them over to collect."

"I'm leaning that way myself," Faith admitted. "Skip seems pretty nervous about them, but don't you think it's strange that they'd come after him here? If he lives in Vegas and they're from Vegas, why would they come all the way to Cape Cod to collect?"

"Unless he's helping them get the entire collection," Midge said, "because the books he owns aren't enough to pay off Mr. Big."

Brooke nodded. "And Derek's probably in with the mob too."

"You don't know that," Faith said.

"Well, I wouldn't be surprised."

Faith shook her head. "All this speculation isn't getting us anywhere. We need facts."

"Which is why I should see what I can find out from the mob guys," Eileen said. "They'll think I'm nothing but a nosy old lady."

"Don't go looking for them. Talk to them only if you just happen to see them around the manor somewhere," Faith warned her. "And stay close to other people when you do talk to them."

Eileen grimaced. "That's not going to be easy since Marlene has basically confined them to their rooms."

"Not that they're staying there," Midge said.

Faith thought for a minute. "I guess it would be a good idea if we mingled with the Drelincourts and the Vegas guys and even the rest of the staff. We'll never figure anything out until we get more information. And we don't need to be deciding who the guilty party is until we have actual evidence."

"Fine," Brooke said.

"Keep out of trouble," Faith told all three of them. "I don't think our thief is dangerous, but you never know how someone will act when desperate."

As part of the plan to mingle, Brooke and Midge went into the billiard room to chat with whoever was in there. If Marlene came along, Brooke would have to go back to the kitchen.

Eileen and Faith headed for the library, pleased to find Mr. Drelincourt and Tilly there, along with Rob, Nadine, Michelle, and—to Faith's surprise—Skip. Tilly had her stack of books sitting close by, Rob kept an eye on his canvas bag, and Michelle's little carry-on was parked next to the overstuffed chair she occupied. At least they were being careful.

"I thought you'd be playing poker with Derek and Lloyd," Faith said to Skip as she took a seat in front of the cozy fire.

Skip shrugged. "It's kind of crowded in the billiard room."

"Crowded?" Faith echoed. There was enough room in the billiard room for all the Drelincourts, the Vegas guys, and most of the rest of the manor staff to fit comfortably, if they were so inclined.

"We came here to see Uncle Max," Skip said. "Not play pool."

Rob raised his brows. "Are you trying to stay away from our uninvited guests?"

Eileen managed to appear only mildly interested, but Faith knew she must be all ears. It was the question they both wanted to have answered.

Skip snorted. "Why would I care about them? They're just two guys."

Faith didn't dare say a word. She didn't mind letting Skip's family ask the awkward questions.

"You did seem to be worried about them," Tilly said. "Is everything okay?"

Skip bent down and fiddled with Petie's collar, not looking at her. "Sure."

"They're not here to collect, are they?" Michelle asked.

Mr. Drelincourt frowned. "What's this about? Are you in some kind of trouble, Skip?"

"Aw, come on, Uncle Max. I swear I don't know anything about them."

"And they just happened to come in from Vegas," Nadine said, absently stroking the sleeping Chihuahua in her lap. "I'm sure everyone in Nevada wants to hurry to Massachusetts and enjoy the beautiful weather we're having."

"Next year," Michelle added, "February in Minnesota."

"I told you I don't know them," Skip snapped. "So lay off."

"What's the matter?" Alice walked into the library, frowning. "Are you all squabbling again?"

"Sit down," Mr. Drelincourt said, dredging up a smile. "It's just more of the usual, and I'm sure there's something more pleasant we can talk about. How's the weather now? I haven't looked outside."

"Not any better." Alice pulled her sweater more closely around herself and sat down. "I want to know about those two men. They're playing poker with Derek and Lloyd, but they were asking about you, Skip."

"Me?" Skip laughed, but his face was suddenly pale. "Why would they ask about me?"

"Stop acting like you don't know," Rob said. "Do you owe them money or what?"

"He's gotten himself in trouble with some mob boss," Nadine said. "I know it."

"You don't know anything," Skip told her. "You don't know anything besides that crazy stuff you teach at college. None of you professors knows anything about how the real world works."

"Now, Skip—" Mr. Drelincourt began.

"At least I know where my next meal is coming from," Nadine said primly.

Michelle smirked. "Even if you do have to eat it alone."

"Quit it," Tilly ordered. "Just quit it, both of you. All of you. If you don't care how you act in public, you could at least be nice in front of Uncle Max. I'm sure this isn't what he wanted when he decided to get us all together."

"Now don't upset yourself, honey," Mr. Drelincourt said. "It's not important."

"It *is* important. You ought to have a nice time after everything you went through to arrange this reunion. I know you would never complain, but they should be more considerate."

Mr. Drelincourt patted her hand.

"She's right." Rob leaned forward. "You seem tired, Uncle Max. Have you had a checkup lately? Lloyd doesn't think you look well."

Mr. Drelincourt laughed. "Those doctors are all the same. Maybe I seem tired because I *am* tired. We had to fight our way through a snowstorm to get here, and things have been a mess ever since."

"Okay," Rob said, "I guess we're all pretty stressed out. But I still think you should have a checkup when you get a chance." He gave Faith an appealing smile. "He's the only uncle any of us has left."

His uncle patted him on the shoulder. "I promise I'll see my doctor when I get home. How's that?"

Rob nodded.

"Meanwhile," Mr. Drelincourt said, "let's enjoy ourselves while we're here. Who knows when we might all be together again? More and more, it seems like we only see the whole family when there's a funeral."

Michelle winced. "Sorry, Uncle Max. We'll try to behave."

"Let bygones be bygones," he said. "Just for a little while. It's going to be a long few days if we can't at least be pleasant with one another."

Nadine nodded, not saying anything.

"Now," Mr. Drelincourt continued, "since the subject has already been addressed, I think we should have an answer, Skip."

"Uncle Max—"

"The truth. Now," Mr. Drelincourt said. "Who are those two men? And why are they here?"

Skip looked faintly guilty. "I don't know. Honest."

His uncle's piercing gaze did not soften. "Who do you *think* they are?"

Skip shrugged.

"The truth."

"I do sorta owe this one guy money," Skip said, staring at the floor.

Faith had suspected as much, though it was certainly helpful for him to admit it. Now maybe they'd make some headway in the investigation.

"I knew it," Nadine crowed.

"That's enough, Nadine," Mr. Drelincourt said, still watching his nephew. "Go on, Skip."

"Well, that's all. I told him I was coming here to see about selling my books and then I'd pay him. I know those two work for the guy I owe, but I don't really know them. I guess he sent them to make sure I didn't do anything with the money besides pay him off."

"You saw the comparables on the list I handed out," Faith said. Now that Skip had finally explained his connection to Mr. Morris and Mr. West, she didn't want to miss her chance to learn more. "Would your books have been enough to pay your debt in full?"

Skip slowly shook his head.

"What if you had the whole collection?" Mr. Drelincourt asked, his voice stern.

"Yeah," he said softly, "I think so."

"Oh, Skip," Alice breathed.

"I didn't take them!" Skip held up both hands. "What do I have to say to make you believe me? I didn't take any books, not even my own."

Nadine glared at him. "I don't care if you didn't take them. You'd better give them back."

Faith saw Eileen bite her lip, maintaining a somber expression even if there was a twinkle in her eyes.

Skip blew out his breath. "Uncle Max, I swear I didn't." His expression was earnest.

Too earnest? Faith couldn't be sure. Evidently no one else could either.

"All right," Mr. Drelincourt said at last, "we'll drop it for now. I *am* tired. I'm going to my room for a while. Try to behave yourselves, and don't cause Faith any trouble. Tilly, Rob, Michelle, take care of your books. We can't afford for any more of them to disappear."

"I won't let mine out of my sight," Rob promised, picking up his bag of books. "And I'll tell Lloyd to stay on his toes. Who knows what Derek's done with his?"

Tilly gathered up her own stack of first editions. "You be careful with yours too, Michelle."

Michelle stood and grabbed the handle on her little carry-on. "Don't you worry."

"Humph." Nadine picked up Mr. Darcy, startling a yip out of him. "I guess I'll go to my room and grade papers if everyone else is leaving."

Skip and Petie wandered out after her.

"I'd better see how Lucy's doing," Alice said.

But when they all left, Rob stayed behind. "Anything I can do to help find out what's going on?"

Eileen beamed at him. "It would be nice to have a real policeman on the case."

"Nothing official, of course, ma'am," he said.

"Maybe Brooke and Midge found out something when they were mingling in the billiard room," Faith suggested, suddenly feeling a little less out of her depth. "We should get together and talk things over and then go from there."

There wasn't much more they could do.

The cat sauntered down the hallway toward the door that had the intriguing female behind it. He still hadn't seen her, but she smelled nice. He'd heard some of the humans talking about a tabby. He liked tabbies, but this one wasn't being friendly at all. She didn't even swat at him when he put his paws underneath her door. Maybe some kind of present would interest her.

Doors. Why humans put so much stock in them, he didn't know. They weren't about to stop him. He knew ways through and around the manor that the humans didn't have the slightest clue about. There was a new one that was very entertaining. How had it escaped his notice until now? It was small, at least compared to the doors the humans typically used, and it was hard to see unless you knew it was there in the back of one of those tiny rooms where they hung their clothes and left their intriguing-smelling shoes.

The first time he noticed it, it was because he'd heard something scrabbling around behind it. Somewhere between the walls. Naturally, his first thought was that there must be some nice, crunchable little mice back there. But the smell hadn't been right.

Even now when he walked into it, it didn't smell like mice. More like those old books his human liked to pet. There was a stack of them inside, piled up like they were waiting to be put away in the library. What was so attractive about them anyway? Maybe they tasted better than they looked.

He opened his mouth to chew the corner of the book on the top of the stack when the door behind him opened.

"Hey!"
The cat knew that voice, the voice of an angry human.
"How did you get in here?"
He darted out the way he'd come and bolted downstairs.

11

Faith, Eileen, and Rob found Brooke and Midge in the billiard room, but no one else was there.

"I see your party broke up too." Faith sat at the table next to Midge and gathered the scattered playing cards. "Any news?"

"Not much," Brooke admitted. "Mr. West and Mr. Morris claim they were on an errand for their boss when the storm hit. Morris is friendly enough, but it's just talk. Hardly any information."

"Yeah," Midge said. "And West doesn't say much at all."

Brooke grinned. "But he won fifty bucks from Derek. You should have seen Derek's face."

"I get the feeling he doesn't have much experience with losing," Faith said. "What about the others?"

"Lloyd had his books with him," Midge told her. "Derek wouldn't say what he did with his."

Eileen thought for a moment. "What about the Vegas guys? They must have said something about Lloyd having a bunch of books with him."

Midge shook her head. "Not really. West moved Lloyd's books when he pulled his chair up to the card table to play poker. I'm not sure why, because they weren't in his way, but he didn't do anything with them. Just moved them over and sat down."

"He could have been trying to see which ones they were," Faith said. "So he could figure what they were worth."

"I guess there are really only two choices here. One of the Drelincourts took the books or one of the Vegas guys." Brooke glanced at Rob. "No offense meant."

"None taken," Rob assured her. "If we're going to get to the bottom of this, it won't do any good for you ladies to tiptoe around me. Say what you think, even if it is about my family. I'm not ruling anybody out yet. And Skip finally admitted he knows who Morris and West are."

Midge's eyes widened. "He did?"

"They work for a man he owes money to."

"Then that's got to be the answer," Midge said. "He stole the books to pay off his debt."

"It could be that," Faith said, "but Skip denies it."

Midge snorted. "Of course he does."

"I still think Derek's in on it." Brooke looked apologetically at Rob. "There's something sneaky about him."

Rob chuckled. "He can be a smooth talker when he wants."

"Don't forget that besides the Drelincourts and the hitmen, there's a third option," Eileen said. "It could be someone who works here."

Faith frowned slightly. "That's a possibility."

"Do you have a suspect?" Brooke asked. "I mean, from the staff?"

"This has to stay strictly between us," Faith said to Rob. "But I guess you're used to keeping information about cases to yourself."

Rob nodded. "I wouldn't keep my job long otherwise."

Faith told them briefly about Marlene's suspicions. "Not that she doesn't have good reason to wonder if it was Laura. And not that there aren't a few things that make me wonder, but she seems so sweet that I just can't believe it of her."

"Looks can be deceiving," Eileen said archly.

"It seems like almost everyone has a motive. At the very least those books are worth a lot of money." Faith ruffled the edge of the deck of cards, considering everything that had happened since the Drelincourts arrived.

They were talking about theft and not murder—thank goodness—but she couldn't help thinking about some of Agatha Christie's works. They were literally closed in at the manor. No getting in, no getting out. Someone among them was guilty. It was like that snowbound train in *Murder on the Orient Express*. Lots of suspects, lots of things that didn't quite fit together, and in the end nothing had been what it had seemed. *And yet . . .*

"Maybe Brooke's onto something," Faith mused.

"I knew it!" Brooke slapped her palm down on the table. "Derek's working with those guys from Vegas. I knew it."

"At this point, anything could be possible," Eileen said. "What if it *is* Derek and the Vegas guys?"

Midge frowned. "But I thought Skip—"

"I have a sixth sense about these things," Brooke interrupted. "Derek's in on it somehow."

Faith rolled her eyes. "Would you leave Derek out of it for a minute?"

Brooke pouted.

"The point is," Rob said, "that we have three classes of suspects. The family, the guys from Vegas, and the staff. Any of them could be stealing the books and hiding them somewhere."

"It would be weird if it was somebody who works here," Brooke said. "I mean, we know everybody."

"But what if it *is* someone on the staff?" Midge turned to Faith. "Yes, we're back to Laura. Is there anyone else at the manor you think is suspicious?"

Faith considered. "No. I suppose we can't actually rule out *anyone* who's in the manor right now, but nobody else on staff has made me wonder. Just Laura."

"Then maybe she should be ruled out," Eileen said. "If you're wondering and Marlene is downright suspicious of her, perhaps you should try to prove that she didn't do anything. Starting with asking her if you can search her room."

Faith was skeptical. "If Laura did take the books, surely she wouldn't keep them in her room. And there are many places in the manor where they could be hidden, especially by someone on staff."

"It would get Marlene off her back for a while," Brooke said. "If Laura *was* silly enough to steal them and hide them in her room, at least you'd know."

Faith got up from the table. "I'll get Marlene, and we'll both check out Laura's room."

"Would you like me to go along?" Rob asked.

The offer prompted a sly look between Eileen and Brooke that Faith could have strangled both of them for.

"That way I could be the bad guy and not you," he explained.

Faith appreciated him trying to relieve her of an uncomfortable job. "It's nice of you, but I'd better go alone. Laura's scared enough of Marlene as it is. If she thought we were reporting her to the police or something, I don't know what she'd do."

Rob nodded. "Plenty of people get nervous around the police and appear guilty when they haven't done anything. Let me know what you find out."

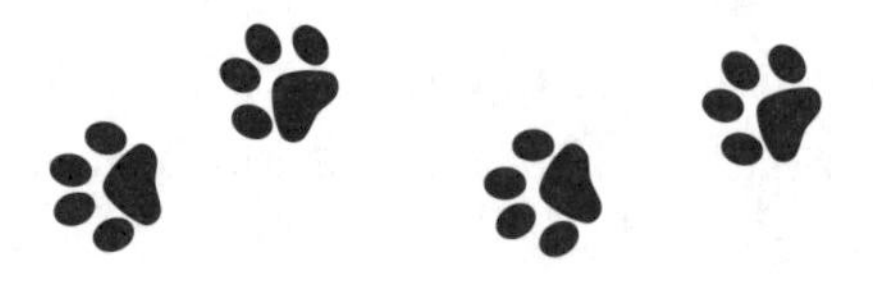

Faith and Marlene found Laura cleaning one of the powder rooms downstairs.

"Are you almost finished?" Marlene asked, inspecting the sparkling-clean room with a critical eye.

"Yes ma'am." Laura wiped her hands on the paper towel she had been using to polish the mirror over the sink. "Is there something you need me to do?"

"We need to search your room." Marlene was never one to mince words.

Laura glanced at Faith, appearing as if she might burst into tears, but she merely nodded, collected her cleaning supplies, and led the way up to her room.

As Faith expected, they found nothing unusual—certainly no autographed Agatha Christie first editions.

But there was a brochure on the bedside table for a university. Marlene picked it up, examined it, and replaced it without comment. She didn't need to say anything. It was for a highly rated and expensive university in Boston.

"Thank you for your cooperation," Marlene said at last. Without another word, she vanished down the hallway.

Laura finally exhaled.

"I'm really sorry," Faith told her. "I know this hasn't been easy for you."

"I just wish you believed me." Laura's voice was tiny and fragile. "I wouldn't do anything like this. I wouldn't steal, especially knowing how important it is for you to get those books for the library."

"Oh, Laura." Faith put one arm around her shoulders. "I don't think you're the type of person to do this kind of thing. But you have to understand how it looks to Marlene. She knows you want to go back to school, especially that school, and how hard it would be on what you earn as a housekeeper. She also wants to tell the Drelincourts we're doing what we can to find the missing books and whoever swiped them. But at least now she knows you don't have them in your room."

Laura managed a tremulous smile. "I guess that's a start."

"We'll figure it out," Faith assured her. "And I do appreciate your trying to help. You could be an extra set of eyes and ears until this is all over."

Laura's face brightened. "I can do that."

"Don't worry about Marlene. Once we find our thief, she'll owe you an apology."

"Yeah, like that's ever going to happen."

"I didn't say she'd ever give you one," Faith said with a grin. "Just owe it to you."

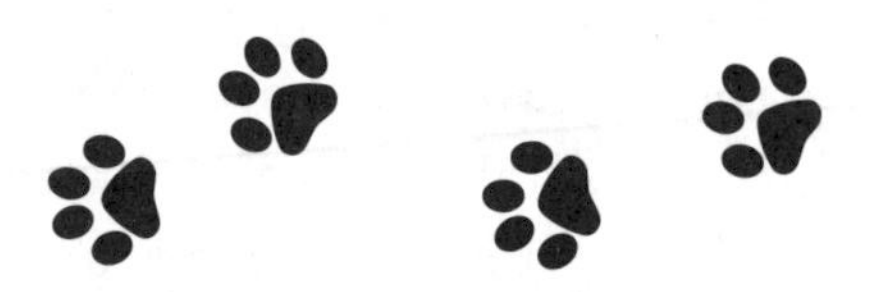

On her way back to the library, Faith noticed Watson sitting in the hallway where the Drelincourt rooms were.

"What are you doing down here, mister?" Before he could get away, she picked him up and cuddled him. "You must be keeping busy since you haven't been following Midge around begging for treats. What are you interested in?"

He answered with a disgruntled squawk.

She glanced over at the door he'd been sitting across from. Alice's room. "So that's what you're curious about." She carried him over to the door and knocked.

For a moment there was no response. Then there was a slight rattle of the doorknob. "Who is it?"

Faith realized she needed a reason to be knocking on Alice's door other than Watson's prompting. "Faith Newberry. From the library. I wanted to check on you and Lucy."

"Oh." There was a louder rattle as the chain and dead bolt were undone, and then the door opened, revealing Alice wearing well-worn sweatpants, an oversize sweater, and thick socks. Her dark hair stuck out in every direction.

"I'm sorry for waking you up," Faith said.

"Not really. Well, sort of. I mean, Lucy was napping." Alice touched Watson's nose. "But then they do most of the time, don't they?"

Faith nodded, peeking around her into the room.

"Lucy dived under the bed when you knocked." Alice stepped back. "Would you like to come in? It's been a little overwhelming for me with everything that's been going on, but maybe you've found out something by now."

Faith didn't have much to go on yet, but she wasn't about to miss the opportunity to have a one-on-one chat with a Drelincourt cousin, especially this one. Alice had been pretty quiet so far, and that probably meant she'd heard a lot.

"Do you think Watson will upset Lucy?" Faith asked. "Should I take him to my room and come back?"

"Can you hold him? Maybe if he doesn't get down, Lucy won't mind."

"I can try." Faith gave Watson a stern look. "You behave or no more tunaroons, got it?"

Watson appeared mildly disgusted.

Faith and Alice sat at the Queen Anne table situated in the bow window of the suite, and Faith settled Watson into her lap. The curtains were closed. There was nothing to see outside but lowering clouds and the endlessly swirling snow.

"I hope you might be able to help me," Faith said.

Alice seemed bewildered. "Help you with what?"

"Castleton Manor would love to purchase the Christie collection, but of course, it's not worth as much if it's incomplete. So I've been doing some sleuthing on my own to try to figure out what's going on."

"I'm sorry, but I don't know anything." Alice twisted her plump fingers together. "I have no idea what happened to my books or any of the others."

"I know, but I'm wondering if you could tell me anything. Anything you've wondered about, anything that's made you suspicious, anything that would give someone a reason to take the books."

Alice wrinkled her forehead. "To tell the truth, we all have some reason or another. But I can't imagine any of us stealing anything. Well, Skip might. He can be a bit fluid in his ideas about what's right and wrong, depending on how badly he wants something. Derek's been in some pretty desperate situations if you believe everything he says, so he might do whatever he thinks he needs to do. About half of us want to sell the books, and the other half would rather keep them in the family."

"Who do you think is in the sell group?"

"Skip definitely. And Derek. Nadine hates the books and would rather have the money to get her own book published."

"I thought she wasn't interested in publication, just in experimenting," Faith said, surprised.

"Oh, goodness no. Nadine's been working on that book for the past twelve years. I think she wants to give up teaching and write full-time if she could afford it. Which she'd be able to do from the proceeds of the Christie books—for a while anyway. From what she says, one of the major publishers will snap it up when it's done. She only says it's not for publication so Michelle won't harass her about it if it never gets published."

"They sure argue a lot, even for sisters," Faith said, making sure her tone was light.

Alice sighed. "It's too bad. They used to be best friends, the kind of sisters who do everything together and enjoy hanging out with each other. And then, not so much."

"What happened?"

"Alex Foxe is what happened. He and Nadine were supposed to get married. In fact they were up to the wedding shower part of the whole process when Alex broke things off. He said he wasn't ready to make that kind of commitment. Two months later, he and Michelle got married in Vegas."

Faith blinked. "Really?" She hadn't known what had occurred between the sisters, but she certainly hadn't expected this.

"The worst part is that it didn't even last a year. He and Michelle had a nasty divorce. She was seeing someone else by then, and he wasn't about to put up with that. She and Alex were never really suited for each other anyway. He was the bookish type, and Michelle always wants to be out doing things."

"How long ago did it happen?"

"It's been, oh, about fifteen years. I think Nadine and Michelle bait each other just out of habit now." Alice sighed again. "I probably shouldn't air the family's dirty laundry, but they make it really hard to have a pleasant get-together."

"Do you think Michelle has any reason to take the books?"

"Not apart from the simple value of them. She definitely wanted to sell, but I don't think she'd steal from the rest of us. Then again, I don't know how her ad agency is doing. She always lives like there's no end to the money, and I can't tell you how much of that is reality and how much is show."

"Anyone else in the sell camp?"

"Eric. He's been struggling to make a living with his books for years now, and his wife told him she's had enough of it and is leaving. Sometimes I wonder if he thinks he could get Lydia back if he had more money. Though what she'd do with her boyfriend at that point, I don't know."

Faith couldn't think of a good response, so she settled for

a sympathetic smile. She hadn't expected shy Alice to be so forthcoming, but sometimes even the quiet ones needed someone to talk to.

"Does that mean the rest of you want to keep the books?" Faith asked after a moment, busying herself with rubbing behind Watson's ears.

"I guess so. I know they mean a lot to Uncle Max, but none of them are his, of course. Tilly wants to keep them for his sake. Rob wants something to leave his boys."

"I understand he's a widower," Faith remarked, carefully nonchalant.

"Yeah. His wife was in a car accident. Rob heard the call over the radio in his squad car and didn't think anything of it. It was only later he found out it was Kelly. That was almost four years ago, and he was pretty cut up over it for a long time, but I think he's finally ready to find someone else." Alice smiled shyly. "He's a good guy. Somebody's going to hit the jackpot with him someday."

"I'm sure. He's helping us figure out what happened to the books."

"I'm glad. I'd rather he did it than the local police. I mean, in case it's one of us. It'd be awful if somebody was arrested."

"You were telling me about who wanted to sell and who didn't," Faith prompted.

"Oh yeah. Well, Lloyd doesn't want the set broken up. He even suggested that we all sign an agreement that when one of us dies, that person's books have to be divided equally among whoever is left until the whole set finally belongs to just one who can sell the collection or leave it to his own heirs. That way the set would never really be broken up. John didn't think it was a bad idea, but he said Jen wouldn't like it."

"Jen?"

"His wife," Alice explained. "They have three kids, and

apparently she wants them to get something from his share of the collection."

"I guess that's a pretty natural way to feel about it. But I understand not wanting the collection to be broken up. It's amazing. I know I'm looking forward to seeing all of it together, and I hope that's soon."

Alice nodded. "I think Jen and Lydia are part of why Uncle Max wanted each of us to come alone. He didn't want us to be influenced by anyone else."

Watson stretched in Faith's lap, and then his ears perked up when a dainty tabby cat poked her nose out from under the bed.

Faith tightened her hold on him but otherwise pretended she hadn't seen. "We'll be calm and quiet," she said to Watson, her voice soft and soothing, "and maybe she'll come out."

Alice gave her a subtle nod. "I guess that's all. As I said, half of us want to sell and half don't."

Faith kept a good hold on Watson. "What about you? What do you want to do?"

"I don't know." Alice looked at Faith, her big dark eyes troubled, then gazed down at her hands, which were folded in her lap. "Davy, my husband, wants to sell. He doesn't understand the books or why I'd want to keep mine. He says if I want them to read, we could buy paperbacks from the secondhand bookstore." She looked faintly apologetic. "Davy's just practical. He's got plans for the money if we end up selling. He figures he could get a lot of things he wants, including a new truck with a crew cab and an extended bed and all the bells and whistles, for what my books are worth." She cringed. "*Were* worth."

"But what would you do if it were just up to you?" Faith asked.

"I'd rather keep them," Alice said, her voice soft. "Not everything's about money, is it?"

"Of course not."

Just then, Faith felt her cat shift in her lap. To her astonishment, Lucy was standing right in front of her, almost nose to nose with Watson. He sat completely still, almost as if he knew any sudden movement would send the tabby skittering out of sight.

"Don't move," Faith breathed.

Alice nodded, a delighted smile on her face as she watched the two cats.

Lucy blinked at Watson. Watson blinked back. Without warning, she bopped him on the nose with one paw and then dived back under the bed.

Faith and Alice burst out laughing.

Watson huffed.

"Well, it's a start," Alice said.

"It was brave of her to come out at all." Faith stood and settled Watson against her shoulder. "Come on, Rumpy. I'll see if I can find you a treat for being such a good boy and for being so understanding." She smiled at Alice when she reached the door. "I'm sure it's hard at first, but I hope she'll see it's not as scary out here as she thinks."

"Maybe." Alice gave her an uncertain smile and shut the door behind her.

12

That evening, Mr. Drelincourt invited Faith and her aunt to join the family for dinner. When they went into the banquet hall, she was pleased to see that Midge and Marlene were also on the guest list and even Wolfe had made an appearance. Unfortunately Brooke had to be in the kitchen working. Somehow Faith ended up between Rob and Wolfe.

"I guess you're stuck with me," Rob said, "but we sleuths have to stick together, right?"

"Right," Faith said lightly.

"I was getting tired of eating upstairs alone," Wolfe said as he pulled out a chair for Faith, though he was looking at Rob with a touch of wariness.

"Well, my goodness," Eileen said, "you should have joined us a long time ago. There's always room for another handsome man at any table, if you ask me."

Wolfe flashed his irresistible grin and sat down. "Thanks for the invitation, Mr. Drelincourt. I hope there haven't been any more problems with the books."

Faith glanced around the table. She had seen Michelle's carry-on and Rob's laundry bag under their chairs when she had taken her seat. Tilly and Lloyd had their copies stacked neatly beside their plates. Derek was being awfully evasive about where his books were, but that was understandable.

"Are your books safe, Derek?" Wolfe asked. "I'd like to know if there have been any other thefts."

"People don't steal from me," Derek said, his expression cool.

Not more than once, Faith thought.

"You're a lucky man then." Wolfe gave him a good-humored toast with his coffee cup, then looked around the rest of the table. "Any clues about the missing books?"

Shivering, Nadine tugged the collar of her heavy cardigan, then made sure Mr. Darcy was warm enough in his own little sweater as he sat in her lap. "I can't wait until this infernal storm is over and the police can get up here."

"What am I?" Rob asked. "Chopped liver?"

"Now, let's not get ahead of ourselves, Nadine," Mr. Drelincourt said. "We'll figure this out, or we'll settle it among ourselves. I don't want a public scandal."

Tilly bit her lip. "I don't want you to upset yourself, Uncle Max."

"Nothing of the sort." He patted her hand. "Don't you worry."

Brooke had managed to put together another delicious meal. This time it was mango-avocado salad on a bed of arugula, baked salmon with tangy dill mustard sauce, diced roasted potatoes and Brussels sprouts, and individual crème brûlées for dessert. The food was served family style, with everyone passing around the dishes and helping themselves.

By the time the last course was consumed, the conversation had gone from the Christie collection and the weather to more congenial subjects like sports and the latest celebrity gossip. Faith wasn't too interested in either, but Midge had plenty to say about the scandalous divorce between one actress and her actor husband, and Wolfe and Tilly had a lively conversation about the Boston Bruins. Then Skip, John, and Derek got into an involved discussion about fantasy sports leagues.

It turned out to be a pleasant evening, especially with Wolfe there to charm their guests and keep everything running smoothly.

When dinner was over, the Drelincourts went their separate

ways. Nadine and Alice planned to go up to Nadine's room so she could teach Alice how to knit. Eric wanted to work on his latest book. Even cut off from her company as she was, Michelle was still working on a bid for her best client.

"Billiards, Rob?" Lloyd suggested. "Derek? Anybody?"

"No, man," Skip said. "I'm going to teach Derek and John how to make a bundle on NFL fantasy leagues."

As usual, Derek was smugly amused. "He claims he is, anyway."

Lloyd frowned. "I don't know why you think he can teach you anything. If he knew how to make a bundle on fantasy leagues, then why is he in trouble with the mob?"

"It'll happen," Skip insisted. "It'll happen."

Lloyd rolled his eyes. "Are you going, Rob?"

"No way," Skip said in a stage whisper. "We can't let the fuzz in on this."

"Hilarious," Rob deadpanned as he grabbed his laundry bag of books. "All right, Lloyd." He glanced at Wolfe and then turned to Faith. "You're both welcome to join us."

There was just the slightest tautness in Wolfe's expression. "Thanks, but I have some business to attend to." His expression relaxed when he looked at Faith. "You should play. With everything that's been happening, you should take a little time to relax."

She shook her head. "I'd love to, but I'm not much of a billiard player."

"How about you, Til? Want to play?" Rob asked.

"No thanks. Not tonight."

"You're not joining them?" Wolfe asked her. "Skip says you're a good player."

Tilly yawned. "Oh, excuse me. I don't know why I'm so tired, but I can hardly keep my eyes open. I think I'm just going to bed."

Lloyd looked her over. "Are you okay?"

"Do you want me to go with you?" Alice said. "I could carry your books."

"No, that's all right. It's sweet of you, but I'm fine. I'm—" She yawned again and turned a little red. "I'd better go before somebody has to carry me." She rubbed her eyes, then gathered her stack of books. "Don't frown like that, Uncle Max. I've been staying up too late the past couple of nights, and now it's catching up with me."

Mr. Drelincourt took her arm. "I'll go upstairs with you. I borrowed *Nicholas Nickleby* from the manor library, and I'd forgotten how much I enjoyed it. I think I'll read awhile and then get some sleep myself. Good night, everybody. See you at breakfast."

There was a chorus of good nights as they left the room.

"I need to work out a schedule for our housekeeping and kitchen staff for tomorrow," Marlene said. "It doesn't look like the storm's going to let up anytime soon, so everyone will have to pitch in as needed."

After Marlene exited the banquet hall, Wolfe turned to Faith. "Are you sure you don't want to play billiards?" he asked, his smile particularly appealing.

Faith shook her head. "Since the four of us are here from the Candle House Book Club, we decided to have our regular meeting." She leaned closer to him, lowering her voice. "Tonight we'll be discussing *The Mystery of the Missing Books*. None of us have finished it yet, so if you'd like to come, you won't be far behind. Maybe together we can figure it out."

"Ah." Wolfe nodded thoughtfully. "I'm sure that's a fascinating story. I'll see if I can stop by once I see to a few loose ends."

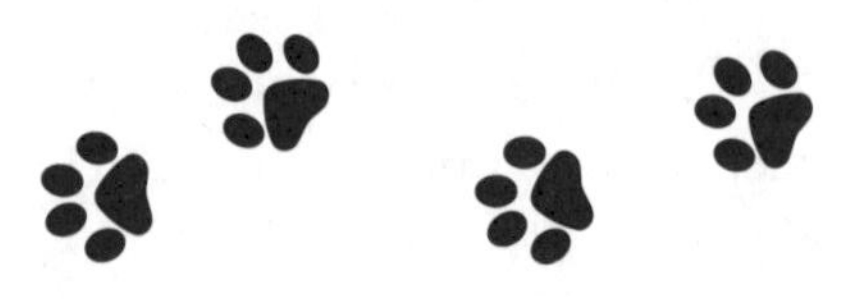

The meeting of the Candle House Book Club proved unfruitful. When Wolfe came down to the kitchen, Faith and the rest of the club members were no further along in the investigation than they had been at the beginning of the evening.

Finally, having polished off their second pot of decaf coffee, they adjourned for the night.

When Faith got back to her room, she found Watson lounging in front of the door, looking rather disgusted by her tardiness.

"And how was I to know you'd suddenly want in, Your Highness?" She picked him up and noticed a little rectangle of cardboard under him.

Watson swiped at it, trying to grab it before he was carried away.

But Faith got to it first. "A bookmark?" she asked, examining it. It wasn't actually a bookmark, though she wondered if it hadn't been used for one. It was a baseball card. No, a hockey card. Bobby Orr, Boston Bruins, 1970. It was signed, *To Jamie, Good luck always, Bobby Orr*. "Where'd you get this?"

Watson squirmed and meowed in protest.

She finally gave him the little catnip mouse she had forgotten she had tucked into her purse before leaving the cottage. She put the hockey card securely inside her checkbook, then fished around for her room key. Once they were inside, she dropped Watson onto the bed. He immediately snatched the catnip mouse and dived under the dresser with it.

Faith sat on the bed and examined the trading card again. It was from 1970. Nearly fifty years old. It had to be worth something, but she had no idea how much. Where in the world had Watson found it? Fortunately, it was still in excellent condition. He hadn't yet chewed the corners off or punched through it with his fangs. It was possible it belonged to one of the Drelincourts. She'd have to ask about it in the morning.

"Don't keep me up all night batting that thing around under there," she told Watson when his vigorous play broke into her thoughts, "or it's going back into my purse."

As usual, he pretended he didn't hear her.

Once Faith had finished her nightly routine and was ready for bed, she pushed her curtain to one side, trying to see what the weather was doing, but the glass was totally frosted over. The moan of the wind and the frequent rattling of ice pellets against the panes told her the storm was not yet over.

With a sigh, she settled into bed with her own not-autographed and not-first-edition paperback copy of *Curtain*, the final adventure of fictional sleuth Hercule Poirot. She could certainly use the help of his gray matter right now. Order and method were his watchwords, but there seemed precious little of either in the case she was dealing with in real life. And there was no use forming theories without facts.

She had just gotten to the end of the seventh chapter and was reaching over to turn off the bedside lamp when there was the softest of knocks at her door. She stopped and listened for a moment, wondering if she had imagined the sound, when it came again. This time it was slightly louder.

Watson poked his head out from under the dresser, blinking sleepily.

Faith threw on a robe she had borrowed from the manor storeroom and went to the door. "Who is it?"

"I'm so sorry to bother you."

Faith recognized the voice and opened the door. "Alice, what's wrong? It must be after one."

Alice was still fully dressed. "I know. I'm sorry. And I'm not really sure what I ought to do."

"What's the matter?" Faith opened the door wider. "Please come in."

"No." Alice's lips trembled. "Thank you, but I can't. I was just wondering, since you work here, if you have a passkey."

Faith shook her head. "That's not part of my job. Did you get locked out of your room?"

"No, but I'm worried about Tilly. She looked kind of funny after dinner, so I thought I'd check on her before I went to bed. I stopped by her room on my way back from Nadine's, but I can't get her to answer the door."

"Why don't we try calling her?" Faith tried to usher Alice into the room.

Alice drew back. "I did try calling her. I tried knocking. I believe there's something wrong, but I don't want to upset Uncle Max or anyone else until I find out what happened. Do you think you could get a passkey? I should have asked the manager, but I didn't know what she'd think, so I decided to ask you."

"It's all right." Faith tied the sash on her robe, then rushed down the hallway toward Tilly's room. "Are you sure she's in there? Could she be in one of the other rooms? Maybe she's talking to Michelle. Or maybe she really wasn't feeling well and went to see Lloyd. He's a doctor, right?"

"Yes. I didn't even think of that. We could check with him."

By then they were at Tilly's door.

"Let's knock one more time," Faith suggested. "If she doesn't answer, we can talk to Lloyd and then get a passkey if we need to."

Alice nodded.

Faith knocked softly on the door.

When there was no response, she knocked a little louder. "Tilly, are you all right?" She glanced around the empty hallway, not wanting to disturb everyone else so late at night, and tapped again. "Tilly?"

"She must be in there," Alice said. "She told everybody she was going straight to bed after dinner."

"Where's Lloyd's room?"

Alice led Faith around the corner to his room and knocked on the door.

After a moment, Lloyd poked his head out. He looked strange wearing sweatpants and a sweatshirt, especially without his thick glasses and with his red hair sticking out every which way.

"What's wrong?" His voice was thick with sleep. "Somebody sick?"

"Is Tilly with you?" Alice asked, peering into his room.

Lloyd frowned. "No. Why should she be?"

Alice told him what she had told Faith. "I think something's wrong. Why won't she answer the door or the phone?"

A moment later, Lloyd knocked on Tilly's door. "Tilly? Are you in there?"

There was no answer.

He turned to Faith. "Maybe you should get a passkey."

Marlene wasn't pleased to be wakened from a sound sleep, but when she heard what was happening, she quickly pulled on a robe. Soon she had Tilly's door unlocked and flung it open.

Still wearing the jeans and heavy sweater she had worn at dinner, Tilly lay unmoving across the wide bed.

13

"I'd say she's been drugged." Lloyd pulled back Tilly's eyelid and shone his little key chain flashlight at her pupil. Then he leaned down to listen to her heart and breathing once more. "She doesn't seem to be in any danger, just deeply asleep. Of course, I'm a hand doctor and my practice is pretty specialized, but I don't think there's anything to worry about. Where are her books, though? Why would someone drug her unless it was for the books?"

A brief search confirmed his suspicions.

"Who could have taken them?" Alice looked at Faith, bewildered. "Who could have done something like that to her?"

"Just like John's dog, Ahnold," Faith said. "Could it be the same drug?"

Lloyd shrugged. "I didn't see the dog, but it's possible. Dogs are sometimes prescribed the same thing for anxiety as people are. Given enough of a dose, it could cause deep sleep for a period of time."

Alice bit her lip.

"What is it?" Lloyd asked warily.

"I take that kind of pill once in a while. I don't actually have a prescription. Davy wouldn't like me to use anything like that. But a friend of mine gives me a few of hers sometimes when things are bad."

He pressed his lips together. "Did you bring any with you?"

Alice nodded.

"How many?"

"A few."

"Has anyone else in the family mentioned taking any similar medications?" Lloyd pressed.

"Nobody's told me," Alice said.

"Have you taken any of yours?" Faith asked. "I don't mean to pry, but if we can tell whether or not you have fewer pills than you should have, it might help us figure out what happened."

Alice glanced at Marlene, then wilted at her disdainful expression. "I took one the first night we were here, but that was all."

"Have you noticed how many are left?" Lloyd asked.

"No, I haven't looked." Alice stared pityingly at the still figure on the bed. "Do you think someone stole them?"

"I think we'd better check," Faith said.

"I'll stay with Tilly," Lloyd offered. "I don't want her left alone right now."

Alice led Faith and Marlene to her room and fetched the toiletry case from her bathroom counter. The pills were in a small plastic bag. There were only five of them.

"Are there any missing?" Faith asked.

"I don't know." Alice pushed one of the pills over to the corner of the bag with the others. "It seems about the same."

"If there weren't many to start with," Faith said, "I don't know how someone could have stolen enough to drug an adult and that big German shepherd."

Marlene shrugged.

"We'll find out more in the morning," Faith said. "For now, try not to worry about Tilly. Lloyd's keeping an eye on her."

Alice didn't seem comforted. "Lloyd's a hand surgeon."

"He's a doctor. He had to get through medical school, so he knows about things besides hands. Now don't worry."

"But keep your door locked," Marlene advised. "Your cousin

obviously didn't take these thefts seriously enough. I know your books are already gone, but hide that medication. In your purse or something. We don't need anyone else being drugged."

"Is Lucy all right?" Faith asked as she and Marlene went to the door.

Alice managed a faint smile. "She scared me earlier. I searched all over and didn't find her. But then I saw her sitting in the window and watching the storm. I guess she has a hiding place somewhere. Right now, though, she's in her usual spot under the bed. She thinks she's invisible, but I saw the tip of her tail sticking out when we came in."

"Well, I think Watson is a little bit smitten, though I'm sure he'd deny it if you asked him."

Marlene cleared her throat. "Perhaps the cat talk can wait until tomorrow."

"Sorry." Faith turned to Alice again. "Are you okay to be by yourself tonight?"

"Oh, sure," Alice said. "And I won't be by myself. I've got Lucy."

"I'm going back to bed," Marlene said, her voice firm. "Faith, you do the same."

Faith managed to not roll her eyes at Marlene's bossiness. "Good night, Alice."

They were going to have to ask a lot of questions tomorrow. So far nobody had really been hurt, but they had to find out who was behind all this before that changed.

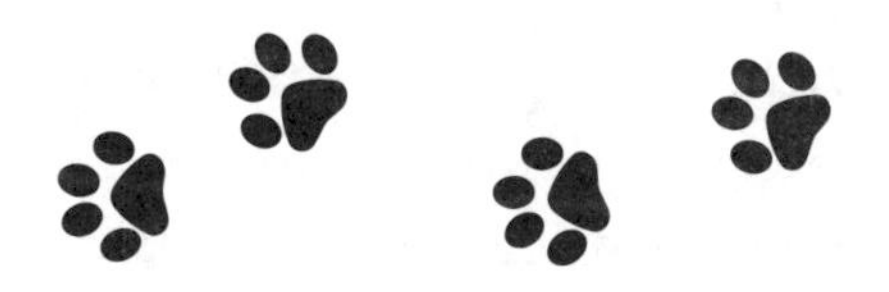

"I just left Tilly's room," Lloyd said the next morning when everyone was gathered for another of Brooke's breakfast buffets.

"For those of you who haven't heard, someone slipped her something—probably at dinner last night—and then stole her books while she was knocked out."

As Faith had expected, that announcement brought on a flurry of questions from everyone at the table, and Rob's eyes met hers questioningly.

Finally, Mr. Drelincourt demanded silence. "Is she all right?" he asked when there was relative quiet.

"She's fine," Lloyd assured him. "She's getting cleaned up and will be down as soon as she can."

"She was drugged?" John stroked his German shepherd's thick fur. "Like Ahnold?"

Midge in turn looked at Lloyd. "Do you know what she was given?"

"I'd say an antianxiety medication. I can't swear to it, of course, not without actual testing, but it seems pretty likely to me."

Midge nodded. "I think that's what Ahnold was given."

Ahnold barked around a mouthful of corduroy cow, and John shushed him.

Faith made a mental note to track down the little stuffed pig Watson had stolen before the dog missed it.

"I'd like to know where the medication came from." Lloyd studied the people at the table. "Are any of you taking something for anxiety? Alice told me last night that she takes anxiety medications once in a while."

The other Drelincourts glanced warily at one another.

All of them except Eric, who was coaxing Don Quixote into eating a bite of scrambled egg. When he realized everyone else was staring at him, he finally looked up. "Oh yeah. I took one this morning before coming down. It, uh, helps when I have to do something stressful."

Like go to breakfast? Faith wondered. But the way some of the others sniped at him and each other, maybe that wasn't hard to understand.

"Did you notice any missing?" Lloyd asked him.

"The bottle's almost empty, but it was that way when I got here. I think there's just one left now."

"But if you take them regularly, won't you run out?" Eileen asked.

"I have another bottle," Eric said as the kitten nuzzled his fingers. "I had it refilled before I left home. I haven't even opened it yet."

Lloyd peered at him. "Is that bottle still full?"

Eric seemed puzzled. "Like I said, I haven't opened it."

"But did you *see* it?" Lloyd prodded. "This morning, I mean."

Eric shook his head. "I assume it's still in my bag with my shaving kit and things. I suppose I should look."

"Might be a good idea," Marlene said, her face grim.

"Take him a minute, will you?" Eric handed Don Quixote to Faith and then stood up. "I'll be right back."

John got up too, along with his dog. "We'll come with you."

The two cousins eyed each other for a moment before leaving the breakfast room.

"So we know Alice and Eric had some of these pills," Mr. Drelincourt said gravely. "Any of the rest of you?"

He was answered with a few head shakes and a few murmurs in the negative.

"No one?"

Again there was no positive response.

"Come along now, Nadine," Michelle said. "Fess up."

Nadine pursed her lips. "I was trying to remember if my prescription bottle was as full as it should be. Don't make it sound as if I have something to hide."

"So you take a similar medication?" Mr. Drelincourt asked her.

Nadine gave him a curt nod.

"I'm sorry to have to ask this, but was your bottle full the last time you checked?" Faith asked, stroking the kitten that was now sleeping against her shoulder.

"No. Maybe half-full. I can't exactly remember. Not close to empty, I'm sure of that."

"She always makes sure there's some on hand," Michelle said.

"Only when I know you'll be around," Nadine replied with a cool smile. She picked up Mr. Darcy from the chair beside her and set him in her lap. "But then who could blame me?"

"Could you two stop, please? It's getting really old."

Everyone turned to see Tilly standing in the doorway. She seemed a little unsteady but otherwise all right.

Lloyd jumped up and helped her to a chair. "How are you feeling? No vomiting?"

"No," she snapped, pushing his hands away. "I'm fine. I just need to eat something."

Her uncle came to her and put his arms around her. "We've been concerned, honey."

She managed a wan smile. "I'm all right. Lloyd says it's nothing to worry about."

Lloyd nodded. "Just make sure you tell me if you notice anything out of the ordinary."

"Whatever good that would do since we couldn't get help here in this weather," Tilly said, shivering.

Michelle beamed at her. "We only wanted to find out if Nadine still has her stash."

Her uncle gave her a withering look as he sat down again.

"You know, I'm really tired of both of you." Tilly helped herself to a piece of toast and started loading it with butter. "Get over yourselves, okay? Neither of you ended up with Alex, and he's better off because of it. If you can't be cordial to each other, at least do it for everyone else."

"We're just trying to figure out what happened to you, Til," Rob said over the astounded and outraged noises the sisters were making.

Alice quietly brought Tilly a cup of tea. "I didn't think you'd want anything strong."

"Thank you." Tilly took a sip, and her taut expression relaxed. "That's good."

"Now what about Nadine's pills?" Skip asked. "I'll go check on them."

"Fine." Nadine dabbed her mouth with her napkin and set it on the table. "Come on, Mr. Darcy."

"You and Petie stay here," Derek told Skip. "I'll see to this." He stood up at the same time Nadine did and caught her arm.

Nadine pulled away from him. "I'm perfectly capable of walking unaided."

"I do beg your pardon." Derek made a courtly bow and opened the door for her and her dog to pass through.

"Do you have any idea how you could have been drugged?" Faith asked once they were gone.

Tilly shrugged. "It could have been anytime. We were passing around serving dishes and our glasses to be refilled at dinner last night. I suppose it wouldn't have taken much to slip something into my food or drink. But I don't believe it was someone in the family." She somehow looked fierce and bewildered at the same time. "Maybe it was done while the food was still in the kitchen. Maybe those guys Skip knows from Vegas got in there somehow."

"But the food was served family style," Rob reminded her. "How could the perp have known exactly what you would be eating?"

"You're the policeman," she told him. "You tell me."

"It wasn't all family style," Brooke, who'd been silent up till now, said from behind the buffet table. "There was crème brûlée. The desserts were each in an individual ramekin."

"But we helped ourselves," Tilly protested. "If the drug was in one of them, how would the thief know which one I'd take?"

"Unless it was someone at the table," Rob said. "Who was sitting next to you?"

"Uncle Max."

Michelle snorted. "You're always sitting next to Uncle Max."

Tilly narrowed her eyes. "Somebody has to take care of him, and I don't see you doing it."

"Yes, I remember he was at the head of the table and you were on his right," Rob said, overlooking the exchange. "Who was on your other side?"

"I—" Tilly gazed down at her teacup. "I don't remember."

"Yes, you do," Alice said, her voice small. "It was me."

14

"I was sitting next to you last night, Tilly." Alice looked miserable. "But I swear I didn't do anything. I didn't put anything in your food or take your books. I didn't."

Tilly put an arm around her. "I know you didn't."

Alice sniffed and nodded.

"And it wasn't Uncle Max either," Tilly said, glaring at Faith. "I don't believe it was anybody in the family. It had to have been those Vegas guys or one of your staff. What about that housekeeper who was in Nadine's room? Was she in the kitchen too?"

Faith thought for a moment. Laura had helped with dinner last night. She hadn't actually served anyone, but she had laid out the place settings and carried a few serving dishes to the table.

"It's got to be someone with a passkey," Tilly said. "How else is this person getting in and out of everyone's room without being caught?"

"I've collected all the passkeys," Marlene said. "None of the staff is allowed to go into any guest rooms alone. And they have to get a key from me beforehand."

"Those are some pretty strong locks and solid doors on our rooms. But a lot of guys on my beat could pick those locks in about fifteen seconds." Rob crossed his arms over his sturdy chest. "Mr. Morris and Mr. West seem like the kind who'd have no problem with that."

"You're set on having those guys involved just because I've seen them around Vegas," Skip said. "But how would they have gotten to Tilly's food? It's not like they were hanging out in the kitchen or anything. Somebody would have noticed."

"One of them *was* in there last night," Eileen said. "Remember?"

Brooke nodded. "As a matter of fact, it was after I had finished up the desserts. He showed up right behind me. Made me jump, I can tell you."

"Neither of you told me about that," Faith said. "Which one was it? What did he want?"

"It was the quiet one. The skinny one. The rest of you were getting the table ready. Eileen was tossing the salad for me, so I guess we were the only ones who saw him. He wanted to know if I had some apple cider vinegar."

"What'd he want *that* for?" Michelle asked.

"I didn't question him about it," Brooke answered. "I poured him a glass, and he thanked me and went away."

"I don't know how that would help him steal books. If that's what he's doing." Faith glanced around the table again. If Tilly's books were gone, that left only four of the Drelincourts who still had theirs. Michelle had her wheeled carry-on beside her. Rob had his laundry bag. Derek had his hidden somewhere. "Where are your books, Lloyd?"

"I got tired of carrying them around all the time, so I took a cue from Derek and found a good hiding place. Don't worry about them."

"I hope it's a better hiding place than Eric or Nadine had for their pills," John said as he and Ahnold came back into the breakfast room.

Eric, Nadine, and Derek were right behind him, their expressions telling the whole story.

Tilly looked slightly queasy. "Their pills are gone, right?"

Derek gave her his usual snide expression. "Nadine's bottle has only about a quarter of what was there before. And Eric's new bottle is missing entirely."

The four of them sat down at the table, and for a while no one said anything.

Faith passed Don Quixote back to Eric, who promptly put the kitten in his shirt pocket to finish his nap.

"So," Faith said, "we know Eric took one of his pills this morning, but it was from his old bottle and not the new one. When did you last take one of yours, Nadine?"

"Yesterday. After my books were stolen. I know I had at least twice as many pills in that bottle as I do now."

"Then your pills couldn't have been used to drug Ahnold."

Nadine shook her head. "I had them after I heard about the dog."

"Maybe our thief didn't realize how many it would take to put a big dog out like that," Lloyd said, "and then thought it would take more to put Tilly under."

"Or maybe this thief isn't through drugging people." Michelle pulled her carry-on closer. "I don't like this at all. How are we supposed to know what's safe to eat or drink?"

Faith looked at Brooke. How could they make sure nothing was tampered with now?

"Don't worry," Brooke said. "From now on we'll serve the meals straight from the kitchen. I'll make sure it's locked up unless I'm in there personally, and nobody will be allowed in except my staff. Then if something else happens, we'll know who to question. How does that sound?"

"All right, I suppose," Michelle said.

"When is this going to be over?" Alice moaned. "I should never have come. Lucy's having an awful time, and I'm too scared to have any fun."

"I'm not scared," Michelle told her. "I keep my books with me all the time, and I sleep with a can of pepper spray by my pillow."

She stared fiercely around the table. "Just in case anyone would like to know."

"I keep mine with me too," Rob said, tugging at his laundry bag. "And I've been trained to defend myself."

Derek leaned back in his chair. "I bet I know where Lloyd's books are."

"I bet you don't," Lloyd muttered.

"I've been in a lot of tight places all over the world, and I know how to find all the best hiding places." One corner of Derek's mouth turned up. "Bet I can find Lloyd's."

"I'm curious," Faith said, trying to defuse the tension between them. "What do you do for a living?"

Derek ran one hand over his thick, dark hair. "I guess you could call me a technology mercenary. I troubleshoot, set up systems, program, whatever somebody needs, no questions asked. For a price, of course. It's usually . . . interesting."

"You act like you're James Bond or something," Lloyd said, his face nearly as red as his hair. "If you're so clever, show me where my books are."

Derek shrugged. "Okay, but I want someone else to come with us. Just so you can't say I didn't take you right to them. Why don't you come, Faith? You're a disinterested third party. Til, you come too."

Faith laughed, startled. "I don't see why not."

"I'll come along," Rob said. "Lead the way."

Derek led them all directly to Tilly's room. She opened the door.

"Where else would you think was a clever hiding place but one of the rooms that had already been robbed? You were in here alone with Tilly last night. You left the door unlocked and came back in to hide your books."

Lloyd looked offended.

"Now this is where it gets a bit trickier," Derek said. "Did you pick the closet? Or maybe under the mattress? No." He grinned and dragged Tilly's suitcase from under the bed. "Where else but here?"

Derek unzipped one side and then the other. His face fell. "I guess I was wrong about the suitcase. What about—?"

"Wait." Lloyd's face was suddenly pale. "They're not in there?"

Derek shook his head, for once without his usual smug expression. "Was that where you put them?"

Lloyd nodded, examining the suitcase himself. "For the reasons you just said." He pushed his glasses up on his head and rubbed his eyes. "I thought nobody would think to look there. What is going on? Who's doing this?"

"Did Tilly know they were in here?" Rob asked as he stalked around the room, flinging open random drawers and doors.

"Of course she did," Lloyd said. "I checked with her first. After what happened last night, I didn't want to upset her, but I thought it was a pretty good idea for a hiding place." He narrowed his eyes at Derek. "You were pretty sure of yourself just now. Maybe they *were* where you said they'd be. Before you stole them."

Derek gave Lloyd a smug grin, but now there was something a little frightening about it. "I'm a lot of things, but I'm not someone who'd steal from his own family."

Lloyd didn't quite look convinced.

Faith definitely wasn't. *Maybe not*, she thought, *but I have no way of knowing that.*

"Instead of assuming someone in the family is behind the thefts, maybe it would make more sense to find out what Skip's friends are up to," Derek said to Faith. "As long as you're pretending to be Miss Marple."

He stalked out of the room, and Rob strode out after him. Faith could hear an argument brewing.

Lloyd shut the door. "Sorry about that. Derek likes to think of himself as a suave, man-of-the-world type, but he's just a programmer. Rob will probably try to make him apologize to you later."

"Do you really think he'd steal from his family?" Faith asked.

Lloyd shrugged. "I'd like to say he wouldn't. I *hope* he wouldn't. But none of us has spent much time with him in years. As far as I know, Derek really has been all over the world, and considering some of the jobs he's done and the people he's worked for, I wouldn't doubt that he's been in some tight fixes. But whether that means he has no compunctions about doing *this* sort of job, I couldn't say."

For a moment neither of them spoke.

Faith wished she could give Lloyd a little hope that his and the other missing books would soon be found. Then she remembered something. "Do you recognize this?" She reached into her pocket, pulled out the trading card, and handed it to him.

Lloyd smiled. "Yeah, I sure do. It belonged to my grandfather Jamison Drelincourt. It's autographed to him. Grandpa loved hockey, and he loved Bobby Orr. He had a framed picture of Orr's famous flying goal on his office wall. 'If it hadn't been for his bad knees,' he always said, 'who knows what ol' Number Four could have done?'" He flipped the card over. "Where'd you get this?"

"I'm sorry to say I found my cat playing with it. He doesn't seem to have chewed it or anything."

"No, it's still in fine shape. I just don't know where it could have come from."

"Maybe someone in the family brought it to the manor. Could your uncle have had it?"

Lloyd frowned as he studied the card. "I suppose it could be any of them. I'll ask around. Mind if I keep it?"

"Not at all. It's yours or at least your family's. I know it's not mine. And it's certainly not Watson's, though I had to give him a catnip mouse in exchange for it."

Lloyd tucked the card into his shirt pocket. "Reminds me of my dog, Bunny. Actually my daughter's, but she's at school, so we're left with the dog. Anyway, good luck getting anything away from Bunny, but she's usually willing to trade."

"I guess she's like most everyone," Faith said, looking out into the hallway where Derek had just gone. "She has her price."

Lloyd followed her gaze. "So you think he'd sell us out if the price was high enough?"

"Maybe anybody would."

"And maybe they wouldn't." Lloyd pressed his lips into a hard line. "Some people think family and tradition are worth quite a lot. But I couldn't say either way about Derek."

"Maybe he's right about seeing what Morris and West have been doing," Faith said.

"You be careful," Lloyd told her. "If you decide to keep investigating, it might be a good idea to take Rob along. He knows how to handle that type."

"I'll make sure to do that."

15

"You want to grill the mob guys?" Rob straightened up and leaned his cue against the billiard table, looking at Faith with a mixture of amusement and admiration in his gray eyes. The game room was empty apart from the two of them.

"I didn't say grill," Faith told him. "But I thought we could see what they know about the missing books. Maybe they don't even know they're missing. Did anyone mention the thefts in front of them? During a poker game or something?"

"Not that I remember, but you're right. They might not have heard anything about the thefts. They must know about the books, though. It seems pretty clear that, at the very least, the books are the reason the two of them are here."

"True." Faith squared her shoulders. "So what do you think?"

Rob grinned and picked up the laundry bag at his feet. "Let's go have a little chat."

When they found no sign of Morris or West on the ground floor, Faith and Rob checked the library. There they were, West glancing around furtively while Morris tried the door.

Faith felt her heartbeat speed up. Was she really about to question two men who were involved in organized crime? She didn't actually know that about them, but she still couldn't help the wobble in her stomach that wouldn't go away. She was glad a police officer was with her.

"Okay," Rob said, his voice low, as he and Faith approached the library door. "I'll do most of the talking, but feel free to ask a few questions here and there."

"All right. You're the expert at this, not me."

"Give them as little information as possible. Just let them talk. And don't tell them I'm a cop."

She nodded and took a steadying breath, then raised her voice. "Mr. Morris. Mr. West. Sorry I wasn't here to let you in."

Morris grinned. "Hey, it's the library lady. We're allowed in here, aren't we? Gord and me get tired of poker and stuff all day."

"Of course," Faith assured him. "You're welcome anytime the library is open. You've met Mr. Drelincourt, I believe."

"Sure, even though the manager doesn't much like us mixing with the upper classes, if you know what I mean." Morris gave a wheezy laugh and then sobered abruptly when Rob didn't join in.

"I'm sorry about Ms. Russell," Faith said, trying to keep from appearing surprised. "She can be a bit heavy-handed at times. You must get cabin fever sitting up in your rooms so much. I can understand why you'd want to mingle."

"Not a big deal. It's just part of her job," Morris said. "Can we look around?"

"Yes. I hope you find something you'd like to read," Faith said. "Is there something in particular you're interested in?"

Rob sat down in front of the fireplace and set his laundry bag between his feet. "I like Hammett. *The Thin Man* is one of the best."

Morris sat across from him. "He's good. Me, I like Zane Grey, but Gordon's more interested in Ibsen."

West nodded and started perusing the nearest bookshelf.

"Funny you two ended up here," Rob said casually. "I know your car went off the road and you needed to get out of the storm, but something brought you out this way in the first place. Was it Skip?"

Morris raised his eyebrows. "Did Mr. Hamilton say he knew us?"

"No, not exactly. He said he'd seen you around in Vegas."

"There's a lot of guys in Vegas."

"He said he owes your boss some money," Rob said. "Is that why you're here?"

"We might have dropped by to check on him since it was on our way," Morris admitted. "No harm in that, is there?"

"I suppose not," Faith said. "Where were you headed?"

"Tallahassee, Florida, ma'am."

West chuckled.

"Lighthouse Bay isn't exactly on a straight line from Vegas to Tallahassee," Rob observed pleasantly.

"It is if our boss says it is," Morris replied. "We're like Ms. Russell, you know? Just trying to do our job."

"Exactly what is your job?" Rob asked.

Morris again raised his eyebrows. "Now you're making us wonder what *your* job is. Why do you want to know?"

"Just wondering. There have been some . . . incidents around the manor. Involving books and things. I wondered if you knew anything about them."

West looked over at Morris, clearly concerned.

"Are you talking about this Agatha Christie collection the boss here wants to buy?" the bigger man asked.

Rob cocked his head. "How do you know about that?"

"You might say we have an interest in it. At least in a portion of it."

"Skip's portion," Faith stated.

"It's our understanding that he made certain guarantees to Mr. Henderson, and we're here to see that those guarantees are honored. Nothing too complicated about that."

"Nolan Henderson?" Rob asked. Obviously he'd heard of the man in the course of his police work. That wasn't a good sign.

Morris nodded. "So what are these incidents you're talking about? Something happen to the books?"

"Some of them are missing," Faith told him.

"Like Skip Hamilton's, am I right?" Morris turned toward his colleague. "I shoulda known."

West shook his head. "Mr. Henderson won't like it."

"We thought you might be able to tell us what happened to them," Faith said.

"Are you accusing us, ma'am?" Morris grinned. "Because if you are, you're barking up the wrong tree. All we're here for is what's owed to our boss. The proceeds from the sale of Mr. Hamilton's books have been promised to Mr. Henderson, and we were sent to make sure they don't get diverted."

"Skip says his books aren't worth enough to pay off his debt," Rob said, "but the whole collection would be."

"Here's the deal," Morris said, leaning closer. "None of them others owe Mr. Henderson anything. So it wouldn't be right for us to count them as part of the payment. At least in our estimation, eh, Gordo?"

"Not part of the deal," West said. "Wouldn't be right."

"What if Skip offered them all to you?" Rob asked conversationally.

"Well, that would be accepting stolen goods," Morris said, "wouldn't it, Officer?"

"Who said I was an officer?"

"You did." Morris chuckled. "Not in words, no, but everything else says it pretty plain. You play poker with a fella, see how he sizes up a room, how he sits, what he keeps his eyes on, you figure it out quick. Probably like you figured us out, right?"

"I guess neither of us can afford to be caught off guard," Rob admitted with something like grudging respect.

"Now that we're all stuck here, Gordo and I would be . . . What's the word Mr. Henderson doesn't like us to be, Gord?"

"*Imprudent*," West said.

"Imprudent, yeah. We'd be imprudent to pull something when there's no way out and not that many people to take the blame. And," Morris added, "when there's an officer of the law hanging around with nothing to do."

Faith glanced at Rob, trying to tell whether or not he believed their story and wondering what he would ask next, but his bland expression told her nothing.

"So," Rob said, "yourselves being excluded, who's your money on?"

"Interesting question," Morris said, tapping his heavy chin. "Could be ol' Skipper thought he could take all the books so he could settle with Mr. Henderson once and for all, but like I said, we couldn't be involved in something like that. Now, if he was to sell the items in question and pay us off in cash, that would be a different matter. We couldn't be held responsible, could we?"

West shook his head.

"Gordon says we couldn't." Morris shrugged. "So there's that."

"And besides Skip?" Rob asked, obviously unconvinced.

"Well, could be anybody in the family, right? That's a tony stack of books if you ask me. Any of them could use the cash. Now that Derek, he'd probably be the fashionable choice in most circles, but me, I usually find it's one of the quiet ones. That writer, what's his name, Gordo? Eddie?"

"Eric."

"Yeah, that's it. Eric. He looks like he'll melt if you stare at him hard enough, but guys like that, the ones who get kicked around all the time, you got to be careful of them. Sometimes it takes just one shove too many and they go off. Know what I'm sayin'?"

Rob nodded. "It happens."

"It would be helpful to let us know if you notice anything suspicious," Faith said.

Morris scratched his ear, considering. "Come to think of it, we did see Derek walking out of the butler's pantry. Didn't have much of a chance to wonder about it at the time, seeing as Ms. Russell swooped down and told us that part of the manor was off-limits."

"Did she know you were in the kitchen too?" Faith asked.

"What?" Morris frowned. "Nah, we weren't in the kitchen. We don't even know where the kitchen is."

Rob pursed his lips.

"You were seen," Faith said.

"Hold on there," Morris huffed. "I tell you we wasn't in the kitchen. We're not even allowed to eat in the dining room when the family is there. Why would we—?"

"I was." West walked back to the group at the fireplace clutching a copy of *Remembrance of Things Past*, his normally bland face pink with embarrassment. "I was only there for a minute."

Morris's heavy brows met over his nose. "You were?"

"For apple cider vinegar," Faith said. "That's sort of a strange request, isn't it?"

"Or just an excuse," Rob added.

"No." West fidgeted with the volume he held, his face reddening a little more. "I needed some."

Rob crossed his arms over his chest. "And why's that?"

West looked down. "I had heartburn pretty bad. I'm not used to eating all this fancy stuff."

Faith pressed her lips together, forcing herself not to smile. *Poor man, he must be intensely shy to be embarrassed over something as common as that.*

"Heartburn?" Rob demanded.

Faith nodded. "It's an old natural remedy. It works for some people."

"You could have told me, Gordo," Morris scolded, then turned to Rob. "I never was in the kitchen myself. That's the truth."

"Nobody mentioned seeing Mr. Morris in the kitchen," Faith said. "How did you even know where it is, Mr. West? It's down in the basement with the laundry. Not exactly something you'd stumble on."

"One of the maids told me where it was since she was in the middle of something and couldn't go," West admitted. "I didn't mean to upset anything."

"You didn't," Faith said. "We just wanted to know why you were there."

"You two were also seen by the Drelincourt rooms and other places that you probably shouldn't have been," Rob reminded him. "Why was that?"

"Just checkin' things out, you know? Seeing who was where and what was what." Morris gave Faith a guileless smile. "Making sure we were in the right place to find our buddy Skip."

"Not helping yourselves to anything that might be left around loose?" Rob prodded.

"Not us," Morris said with a grin. "That would be imprudent."

"So what do you think?" Faith asked Rob once Morris and West left the library with the books they had selected. "Are they telling the truth?"

"Hard to say. Are you sure about this apple cider stuff?"

"Oh yes. I've tried it a couple of times myself. Sometimes it works, but the cure may be worse than the disease."

Rob grinned. "Maybe he wasn't lying. About that anyway."

"I thought it was interesting that they saw Derek coming from the butler's pantry. What could he have been doing there?"

Rob patted his ever-present laundry bag. "He said he had a great hiding place for his part of the collection. Maybe the books are in there somewhere."

"Could be." Faith sighed. "The manor's a big place. His books could be anywhere, along with the rest of them."

"Faith?" Marlene entered the library. "I'm glad to find you too, Mr. Drelincourt. You're a policeman, I understand."

Rob nodded. "Something wrong? I mean, something besides the books."

"The cell phones aren't working anymore for some reason. Not that we could get any help out here if we needed it."

"At least we have a doctor, a vet, and a policeman stuck with us," Faith said, trying to look on the bright side.

Marlene gave her a sour smile. "You might also be interested to know that one of our passkeys is missing."

16

"Missing?" Faith glanced at Rob, then back at Marlene. "How do you know?"

Marlene was obviously exasperated. "I didn't actually count the passkeys I collected from the staff until just now. I don't know why it never occurred to me, but I guess since I'd taken them from everyone who's snowed in with us who's *supposed* to have one, I didn't consider there still might be one more out there somewhere."

"How do you know there is?" Rob asked.

"It's my *job* to know how many keys there are," Marlene said. "When I found out I was one short, I called everyone on staff who would usually have a key to see if someone had taken a key home by accident. No one did."

Faith frowned. "How did you call around if the cell phones aren't working?"

"That's *how* I found out the cell phones aren't working. I was talking to one of the housekeepers, the last one on my list, thank goodness, and the line went dead. I tried to call back, but there's no signal whatsoever."

"Great. We really are cut off now, and we're no closer to locating those books than we were on day one." Faith noticed that Laura had come into the library, so she lowered her voice. "How many people still have their books?"

Rob patted his laundry bag. "Me, of course. Derek's got his squirreled away somewhere. Michelle totes hers around with her all the time. That's it."

Faith shook her head. "Where does somebody hide that many books? And how does this person expect to smuggle them all out once the roads clear?"

"Maybe I'll check on Michelle's books just in case," Rob said and walked out.

"I finished everything on my housekeeping list, Ms. Russell." Laura approached Marlene and Faith, her arms loaded with books that needed to be reshelved. "I thought I could finish up in here now."

Marlene frowned. "Everything? And there's nothing Miss Milner needs you to help with in the kitchen?"

Laura seemed bewildered. "I didn't ask her. I thought—"

"You'd better go see," Faith told Laura, glad to have an excuse to get her out of the room until she was through talking to Marlene. "I'll take care of the books."

Laura set the books down and left.

"So what are we going to do?" Marlene asked. "The thief can get in and out of just about anywhere with a passkey."

"Anywhere but the manor itself," Faith reminded her.

"As long as the ice doesn't melt."

"Until then, we keep looking."

"And hope the thief doesn't decide to use those stolen pills on anyone else." Marlene exhaled. "I need to find out about the phones and make sure the generator is good for at least another couple of days. We can't have the reputation of Castleton Manor damaged because of this. Figure it out." Not waiting for a reply, she swept out of the library.

Faith remained seated. *Figure it out?* Fine. But she didn't have to do it alone.

A few minutes later, the members of the Candle House Book Club were seated around the big table in the library. Wolfe had agreed to join them.

As succinctly as she was able, Faith went over the most recent events, including the conversation she and Rob had had with Morris and West.

"Do you think they're behind it?" Eileen asked. "You should have let me talk to them."

Faith couldn't hold back a touch of a smile. "Thank you, but we handled it just fine."

At the word *we*, Wolfe set his jaw, almost imperceptibly, but his expression remained neutral.

Faith decided to ignore it and continued. "I don't know what to think of them. They're working for someone who seems shady. They seem to realize they would be the prime suspects in any criminal investigation and want to stay out of trouble, though they do admit to coming here specifically to make sure Skip pays them whatever he gets from the sale of his books."

"Suppose we rule them out for the time being," Brooke said, "because they're obvious."

"And the staff," Midge added. "At least for now."

Means, motive, and opportunity, Faith thought, *and Laura has all three*. "I think we should concentrate on the Drelincourts. Who are our most likely suspects? Besides Derek," she added when Brooke started to say something.

"Diva and Bling wouldn't like him," she protested.

"They all have a motive," Wolfe said. "The money. Everybody has a reason to want more money. The difference is that some of them might be willing to cross the line to get it."

"That's a good place to start." Midge thought for a moment, twisting a lock of hair around one finger. "Skip would be the one with the most obvious and urgent need for money, judging by the Vegas guys."

"Agreed," Faith said. "Who else?"

"There's Eric," Eileen said. "I've heard he'd do just about anything to get his wife to stay. 'Just about anything' usually takes money."

"Nadine wants to quit her job," Midge said. "And if she means to get her book published, I'm sure she won't want it to be by some obscure university press. If she can't get a big-name publisher to take it and decides to publish it herself, it'll cost her for editing, cover design, and promotion. I can't see her standing for anything less than the best. Not if she's going to show up Michelle."

"Michelle has a motive, doesn't she?" Wolfe leaned forward, his fingers laced together on the table. "What do we know about her company? The economy's been tough lately. Maybe she needs cash before it goes under."

Brooke propped her chin on one hand. "Too bad the Internet's down. We can't even check on her. But I still think it's Derek."

"Maybe it *is* Derek," Faith said suddenly. "And Skip. And Nadine and John and Tilly and even Mr. Drelincourt."

Wolfe's face showed rare surprise. "What?"

"What if it's not *one* of the Drelincourts," Faith said, "but two or more of them? And the squabbling and sniping at each other is just to make us think they're always at each other's throats when really they're working together to mislead everyone else."

"But why?" Eileen seemed thoughtful.

"The books, of course," Faith said. "The collection is valuable. Being snowed in together like this, I can't help thinking of *Murder on the Orient Express*. They were snowed in on a train, and Poirot had so many conflicting clues that he didn't know what to think. Then he realized the culprits were covering for each other, making it appear that nobody could have done it when they were actually in on it together. What if that's what some of the Drelincourts are doing?"

Midge's forehead wrinkled. "But they already have the books. Or had them. Why would they all steal them from themselves?"

"Good question," Faith said. "I'm just thinking out loud. Why *would* someone steal from himself?"

"Insurance," Wolfe offered. "That would be the most common reason."

"Perhaps they want to blame the thefts on our staff so they can sue the manor." Midge looked at Wolfe. "Everyone knows you've got money."

"Some people make a living by filing nuisance suits because they know it can be cheaper for the other party to pay them off rather than take matters to court, even if the case is ridiculous." Wolfe made a wry face. "Ask me how I know."

Midge winced. "But they haven't made any accusations, have they?"

"Well, Nadine has accused almost everyone, including her own family," Faith said. "Marlene is sure Nadine will sue if her books aren't returned. Mr. Drelincourt tries to keep her and everyone else in his family calm, but he doesn't seem to have much effect. What do you all think of him?"

Eileen flashed a mischievous smile. "I think he's quite an attractive man."

"There's more than one of those around here," Brooke added, smirking at Faith.

Faith glared back at her.

"I think he's not well," Midge said. "I know I'm an animal doctor, but he just doesn't look right to me."

"I've thought that too," Faith said.

"Maybe he needs a terribly expensive experimental treatment or something," Brooke suggested. "That would make him desperate enough to steal."

"But would he steal from his own family?" Eileen shook her head. "Wouldn't he ask them for help if he needed it? They all seem to like him pretty well. Surely they'd be willing to sell the books to get him treatment."

"He's pretty crazy about his nieces and nephews," Midge said. "I can't imagine him stealing from them under any circumstances."

"Me neither," Faith said. "But I can't help wondering how he must feel about the first editions. You can tell they mean a lot to him. What if he expected to inherit them when his father died and felt slighted when they were left to his nieces and nephews instead? He can see they don't care about them except for the monetary value."

"But some of them don't want to sell," Wolfe pointed out. "I don't get the impression that John does. Or Lloyd or Tilly or Alice."

"Alice doesn't want to sell." Faith remembered Alice's worried eyes as she talked about the books. "But she knows her husband wants her to."

"What about Rob?" Wolfe asked, a sudden coolness in his expression. "You've spent a little time with him, especially when you were questioning the gentlemen from Vegas. What's your impression of him?"

"He seems like a pretty straightforward guy who wants to keep everybody and their property safe. I'd imagine that he's a good policeman." Faith shrugged, not wanting to give them the idea that there was something between her and Rob. "But that would still be a guess. Maybe he's just a good actor. He's certainly not letting his own books out of his sight."

"That makes him smarter than everyone else except Michelle," Brooke said.

"What about Derek?" Midge asked. "He still has his books."

"He *says* he still has his," Brooke said firmly. "He could end up just like Lloyd and think he's got them hidden and then find out they're gone."

"I thought you were sure Derek was behind this," Faith teased.

"Until his books turn up missing," Brooke said, "my money's still on him. But I want to know how someone got one of those passkeys. That means none of us is safe anywhere."

Wolfe was grave. "I'm assuming it was taken the night the Drelincourts arrived. Or possibly before. It seems likely that the thief used it to get into the rooms where the first books were taken. Tell me again whose those were."

Faith thought for a moment. "Skip, Alice, and Eric."

"I'm sure someone had the passkey by then," Wolfe said. "The easiest way to get one would be to pick one of the housekeepers' pockets. But she'd have to know pretty quickly that it was gone and report it. Marlene hasn't mentioned that to me."

"She didn't say anything like that to me either. I know they keep spares at the front desk, but only someone on staff should have been able to get to them."

"Maybe our thief has an accomplice who works here," Midge said, clearly not liking the idea.

"We can't rule that out yet," Faith said. "Unfortunately."

Just then there was a knock. The library door opened, and Rob stuck his head inside. "Hey, I heard you were meeting in here, and I wondered if I could join you."

Wolfe nodded and pushed out a chair for him. "Any news?"

Rob plopped his laundry bag on the table and sat down. "Nothing yet. But I checked on Michelle. She still has her bag of books with her, and I pity anyone who tries to take them away. I wish Lloyd had been smart enough to keep his with him. That seems to be the only way to thwart the thief."

"Oh, did Lloyd ask you about the trading card?" Faith asked.

Rob frowned. "What trading card?"

"He said it was your grandfather's. Bobby Orr from 1970."

"What? Where'd Lloyd get that?"

Faith cringed. "I'm afraid my cat had it. He must have found it somewhere and carried it up to my room."

"I don't think so." Rob fumbled with the drawstring on his laundry bag. "It was in my copy of *Evil under the Sun*, and I thought it was pretty cool that it ended up in one of my books. How would your cat have gotten it?"

"Could it have fallen out when we examined the books?" Wolfe asked, leaning over and peeking into the laundry bag as Rob opened it.

"Somebody would have seen it," Rob said, pulling out one of his books and quickly opening the brown-paper wrapping. "I would have—" He stopped short, his lips pressed into a hard line. Then he pushed back the paper so everyone could see the contents.

It was a copy of Daphne du Maurier's *Rebecca*.

17

"Great." Rob shoved the book across the table to Faith, then tore the brown-paper wrappings off the other books in his laundry bag. Besides the du Maurier, there was an eclectic assortment of authors and genres. Bradbury, Hemingway, Brontë, Kafka—anything, it seemed, that would approximate the size and shape of the Christie first editions.

Faith opened the cover of one and then two others. "They're all from our library."

Scowling, Wolfe snatched one up, examined it, and thumped it back onto the heavy table. "Did you leave your bag unattended anywhere? Even for a minute?"

"Only in my room. While I was there," Rob said. "They had to have been switched out when I was sleeping or in the shower. That stupid passkey."

"When was the last time you actually saw the books?" Faith asked. "The Christies, I mean."

"When I put them in here." Rob ran one hand over his short hair, thinking. "I've been carrying them around all this time. I never thought to check them."

"You put them in there yesterday after Nadine's books were taken?"

Rob nodded, looking disgusted. "Some cop, right?"

"Nobody in your family came into your room for anything?" Wolfe asked, his blue eyes hard. "Not even for a few minutes?"

"No."

"Not Skip? Or Derek?"

Rob shook his head. "Nobody. Whoever the weasel is, he's good." Nobody seemed to know what else to say.

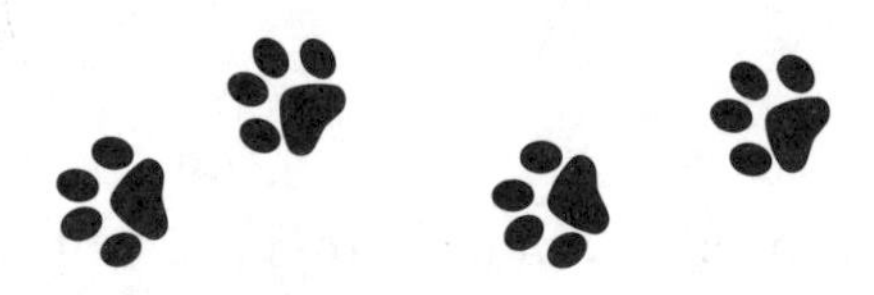

Footsteps woke the cat from his nap behind a potted plant. It was a human carrying one of those bags they put clothes in when the other humans were through wearing them. It seemed a shame to wash them when they were just beginning to have entertaining smells, but humans seemed pretty much set on doing it anyway.

He followed the human through the corridor and down to the room where humans washed their clothes. The human unlocked the door, and the cat darted in afterward, careful to keep from being seen. He almost never got to come in here, and when he did, he was usually escorted back out in short order. Maybe this time he'd have a few minutes to snoop around while the human was busy with the big boxes of stinky powder.

But it was only a few.

Soon there were more footsteps coming down the stairs, and then he heard two humans talking. One of them was his own human's aunt. She gave good belly rubs and back scratches. The other was the human who brought him tunaroons that almost, but not quite, made up for her being the same one who gave him undignified examinations.

The human with him in the room froze, waiting for them to go by. When everything was quiet again, the human eased the door open, stepped outside, and pulled it closed. But not all the way. Good, because once the cat was finished with his explorations, he wasn't about to stand around yowling until somebody let him out.

Not wasting a moment of his unexpected opportunity, the cat investigated what the human had been doing. He didn't like walking on the little bits of the powdery stuff that had fallen on the floor. It poked the pads on his feet, reminding him of when his human had foolishly put the wrong kind of litter in his box. But he didn't let the discomfort keep him from inspecting that part of the room.

He tugged at the cabinet door the human had opened earlier, but it was firmly closed. Even rolling onto his back and pulling from the bottom—always successful when he was at home—did no good. Displeased, he examined the shelves along the far wall. Besides some folded cloths with tantalizing strings, like the ones his human's friend wore in the place where the food was, there was nothing interesting.

Disappointed, he decided to go back up to the main floor. Maybe he could find the human with the tunaroons. He turned and trotted toward the door and then stopped. It wouldn't be a proper investigation if he didn't peek inside the trash can. Though why the humans called them trash cans when they usually had the best stuff inside, he didn't know.

The cat put one paw on the rim of the metal can and pushed, but it didn't turn over. Fine. He rose on his hind legs and braced his front paws on the edge of the can. He could see it was practically empty, but there was one thing in there that might be of interest.

Leaning in as far as he was able, he batted at it and managed to catch it with his claws and bring it close enough to bite it and yank it out of the trash can entirely. He flicked it across the stone floor until it skittered under the shelves and he had to fish it out again. That was a fairly entertaining game, so he did it several more times before carrying his prize to the door.

He patted the side of the door, but it didn't move, so he was forced to turn his paw over and pull from the bottom. That made the door swing open wide enough for him to slip through and out into the hallway, his souvenir in his mouth.

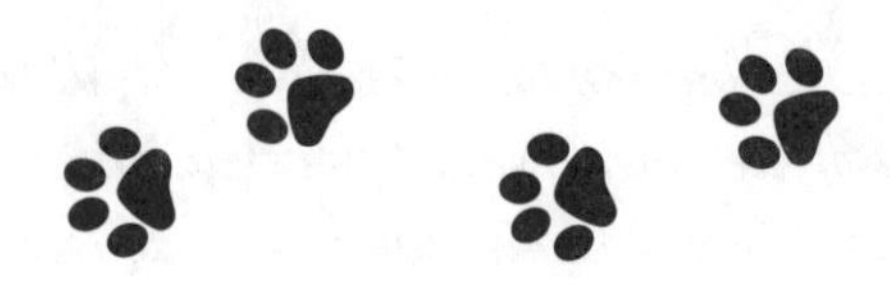

Once Rob had realized his part of the collection was gone, he called the rest of his family into the library.

As usual, no one admitted knowing anything about the books. No one had an alibi for every moment of the time that had passed since Nadine's books were taken. They all slept in separate rooms, so any one of them could have crept out in the middle of the night and used the passkey to get into Rob's room and substitute the library books for the Christies.

"Come on," Rob insisted. "I would have noticed somebody coming into my room, taking out my books, replacing them with the other books, and then getting out and locking the door afterward. No way I would have slept through all that."

"You would if somebody gave you some of that medication." Tilly's voice was soft, but there was something piercing about it, something that reflected the uncertain fear in her wide-set eyes.

Faith could understand her fear. It would be creepy to realize you'd been drugged and completely defenseless and that you didn't really know what happened when you were out or whether it would happen again.

Faith looked around the table, studying each of the Drelincourts in turn, stopping at Rob. "Could you have been drugged? How did you sleep last night?"

"Fine. Like always. That doesn't mean I wouldn't have noticed if someone came into my room." He frowned at Tilly. "Or if I was drugged."

Tilly merely looked uneasy.

"You never had that bag out of your sight?" Wolfe asked.

Rob shook his head. "I told you, except when I was sleeping or showering."

"Someone came into my room when I was in the bathtub," Nadine said.

"I shower," Rob told her firmly, "but I would have heard somebody come in even through the running water."

"How late were you up last night?" Faith asked. "Is there any possibility someone could have given you even a small amount of that drug and you just slept it off?"

"I don't think so." Rob turned to Lloyd. "How long would it take to affect me?"

"It's hard to say exactly. So much depends on the dosage and the recipient. Do you remember when you last had something to eat or drink last night?"

"Yeah, it was at dinner. Probably eight or so?"

Several of the Drelincourts nodded.

"I didn't have anything after that. I played pool awhile," Rob continued. "Sorry, Lloyd, *billiards*. Lloyd and I played awhile, and then I went to bed. What time do you think it was, Lloyd? Eleven? Twelve?"

Lloyd seemed to consider. "I think it must have been closer to twelve. I had my books with me. You had yours. Nobody else came into the room."

Rob nodded. "There was no way I could have been drugged and no way somebody could have come into my room later on."

"I'm not going to let the same thing happen to my books." Michelle thumped her carry-on onto the table and swiftly unlocked it. Then she turned back the wrappings on some of the volumes. "Whew. They're still here. They're fine."

"Just you and me, babe," Derek said, appearing as if he might laugh. "We need to look out for each other."

Michelle eyed him coldly as she snapped the case and locked it again. "I'll look out for myself, thank you."

Now Derek did laugh, but he was the only one.

"What about your own books?" Mr. Drelincourt asked, his expression wary. "Are you sure they're safe? Maybe you should move them from wherever they are so someone doesn't find them."

"Don't worry, Uncle Max," Derek said. "They're perfectly safe. Nobody steals from me."

But do you steal from others? Faith wondered.

"Whoever's been taking the books," Mr. Drelincourt said, his gaze darting almost imperceptibly to Skip, then to Alice, Eric, and Tilly. "They're not worth the trouble you'll cause yourself and all of us by stealing them." He glanced at Derek, then looked beyond all of them and into the flickering library fire. There was something sad in his expression. Regretful.

When the impromptu meeting finally broke up, with none of them any wiser than before, Faith touched Mr. Drelincourt's arm. "Would you please stay and talk to me for a few minutes?" she asked.

Everyone was filing out of the library, but Tilly turned back. "Are you coming, Uncle Max?"

"In a minute, honey. You go on."

Tilly nodded and shut the library door, leaving Faith and Mr. Drelincourt alone in the cavernous room.

"What can I do for you?" Mr. Drelincourt asked.

"I just wondered if you had any thoughts about who might be behind this business with the books. I don't like to ask, but do you think it could be one of your nieces or nephews?"

"No, of course not." He smiled. "I know how it looks, but no. Have you ruled out those two men from Las Vegas? I can't imagine it would be someone on your staff."

"Truth is, we can't rule any of them out. Just like we can't rule out anyone in your family." Faith watched his eyes. They remained troubled, but there was no discernible change in reaction to her words.

"Maybe," Mr. Drelincourt said after a moment, "we should forget about Mr. Jaxon buying the collection. I don't want him or you worrying about the books. Obviously you can't be expected to buy something we no longer have in our possession. We'll find them and take them all home with us. I'm sorry my attempt at getting the family together ended up setting them at each other's throats." He sighed. "I should have known better. My father thought they'd squabble over the collection, but he hoped splitting the Christies among them would keep them together at least in some way. It didn't work."

"Why didn't he leave them to you?" Faith asked. "Wouldn't that have been simpler?"

"I don't know if it would have been," Mr. Drelincourt admitted. "I would eventually have left them to my nieces and nephews anyway. The only upside would have been that I wouldn't be around to see them fighting over them."

"There's no one else you'd want to have the books?"

Mr. Drelincourt shook his head. "Though I wouldn't have minded them ending up here." He gazed around the library, admiring the bookshelves that went up two levels. "At least they would have been kept together and been properly cared for, and my family would have had the proceeds. Now—" He made a little popping sound, like a bubble bursting. "Now no one gets any benefit out of them."

"And if your father had left them to you?" Faith asked.

Mr. Drelincourt appeared wistful. "I would have kept them all. Have you thought about it much? Those books were collected by my grandfather across six decades, and he made sure each of them was autographed. I don't think there's another collection like it, not one where each book was purchased by the same person as they were released. It can't be duplicated, and it can't be replaced. I didn't want the books to be split up, which I suppose they would have been anyway unless someone like you bought the entire collection. But now, unless we find them all, the set is ruined. I can't help thinking that we would have been better off if we had stayed home." He looked sad and tired.

"I still hope we'll find out who has them," Faith said. "And maybe we can still buy them for the library and keep them all together. But what if we do find out that one of your nieces or nephews misappropriated them? What would you do?"

"I don't know. I think I'd rather just drop the whole matter. Though I don't suppose the others would let it go without getting their property back."

Faith smiled sympathetically. She didn't think so either.

18

The cat carried his prize carefully up the stairs and then darted behind the potted plant where he had napped earlier. For some reason, whenever humans saw him with some of the best playthings, they tried to take them away from him. It didn't make sense. They never seemed to want to play with them themselves. And they were often grouchy or even alarmed when they saw him with something new. So he had learned to keep the best prizes to himself, at least at first. That way if a human seized it, he would have already gotten some fun out of it.

He batted the prize around behind the pot for a few minutes, leaping straight into the air and then pouncing down on it, making it skitter around. Then he caught the end of it in his teeth and carried it across the floor.

"What do you have, Watson?"

At the sound of his human's voice, the cat lowered his head and bolted toward the stairs.

"Watson!" His human ran to the foot of the stairs, blocking his way.

Should he go back the way he'd come or dive into the room with the velvet-covered table and those balls that he sometimes pushed around on it?

The instant of indecision cost him his freedom. He heard a chuckle from behind, and suddenly he was lifted off the floor and carried away in a most undignified manner by the big human who lived on the third floor.

"Got you," the human said, grinning.

The cat didn't think there was anything to grin about.

His human came over to the big human and took the cat in her arms. "Little rascal," she said, cuddling him close. "What do you have now?"

He scowled at her, but that didn't make her put him down. Instead she started examining his prize.

"What is it?" the big human asked.

"Some kind of pull strip. Off a box or something. Does it seem familiar to you?"

The cat squawked in protest when the big human filched his prize from him.

"This is a long strip. If it's off a box, it's a pretty big one. Something industrial or commercial, I'd think."

The cat swiped at the strip with one paw, trying to snatch it back.

The big human laughed and roughed up the fur on top of the cat's head. "Hold on a minute." He studied it for a moment and then let the cat take possession again.

His human set him on his feet. She didn't even take his prize from him. "Go on. It's all yours."

He raced away. Nobody had to tell him a second time.

As Watson scampered off carrying the pull strip, Laura walked by. She stopped and watched him go. "So it was Watson, was it?"

"What's he been into now?" Faith asked her.

"I was down in the laundry room a little while ago, and I noticed one of the new boxes of detergent had been opened. One of the big ones. Some of the detergent was scattered on the floor and around the shelves and machines. I didn't know who would have been in there, but now I get it."

"I don't understand why Watson would be in the laundry room," Wolfe said. "It should be locked or at least shut up. Our staff would know that. An outsider might not think to shut the door after himself. Or herself."

"Maybe we should check it out," Faith said.

Faith, Wolfe, and Laura hurried across the lobby, through the butler's pantry, and down to the laundry room. Sure enough, there was a huge box of detergent with a top that flipped back once the pull strip was removed. As Laura had described, there was detergent scattered on the cement floor. There wasn't much of it but enough to indicate that the box had been recently opened and the contents disturbed. The box was maybe half-full.

"Let's pass over how Watson got in here in the first place," Faith said. "He obviously stole that pull strip and carried it off. But if this box was opened recently enough for the strip to still be around, then what happened to the rest of the detergent? Or are the boxes usually not completely full to start with?"

"They're not filled to the top," Laura said, "but they're not this empty. Not when we first open them."

"That much wouldn't have been used in the past day or two, would it?" Wolfe asked, inspecting the box and then the shelves that lined the back wall.

Laura shook her head. "We haven't been running the washing machines. Ms. Russell said we'd better not use that much power because we don't know how long we might be snowed in. She doesn't want the generator to give out. We don't have many guests staying, so we've been using the clean towels and linens we already had stocked up before the storm hit. But even at our busiest, we wouldn't use this much detergent in only a couple of days."

"What would someone do with that much detergent?" Faith

mused, trying to come up with some connection between it and the missing books. "If it has anything to do with the stolen first editions, what would the thief have used it for?"

Wolfe grinned. "Maybe once he sells the books, he wants to launder the money."

Laura giggled.

Faith rolled her eyes but smiled. "Everyone's a comedian."

Wolfe opened the cabinets and then leaned over the deep double sink in the corner. "Hmm."

"What'd you find?" Faith asked, going over to him.

"This may be our answer." He pointed to the thick, pasty film around the drain opening and a few corresponding streaks at the bottom of the sink.

"The detergent was dumped down the drain," Faith said. "Which means something else was put in its place."

Wolfe nodded. "Something that's not there anymore."

Faith went back over to the half-empty detergent box and peered inside. "It couldn't have been the stolen books. There are dozens of them missing now."

"But it would hold a few of them quite nicely." Wolfe sized up the box and the amount of detergent left in it. "Maybe our technology mercenary isn't quite as clever as he thinks he is."

Laura appeared puzzled for a moment, and then something clearly dawned on her. "One of the guests asked me about getting some of his laundry done, and I told him we weren't doing any of it until the regular power came back on. Do you think—?"

"Which one was it? Derek? The tall, good-looking one?" Faith glanced at Wolfe, wishing she hadn't added that last part. Things were awkward enough about Rob already.

Laura nodded. "It was right after the one with the Chihuahua got her books taken. After, well, you know."

After she had had her room searched. Faith still felt bad about that.

"He must have thought his books wouldn't be found in here." In two long strides Wolfe was at one of the washing machines, throwing it open and then doing the same for the others and the dryers. "Empty." He sighed. "I guess it was possible."

"I don't know why we hadn't thought of it before," Faith said. "I wish you'd been right. If he did actually have them hidden in the detergent, I hope they were really well wrapped. I'd hate to think of the damage those chemicals could have done to them otherwise."

"I wonder what happened to Derek's books now," Laura said.

"Maybe he moved them," Faith said. "The guys from Vegas told me they saw him leaving the butler's pantry. I'm assuming that was when he was hiding or moving his books. I'll have to ask them if they remember specifically when that was."

"Or maybe he *did* have the books in the washing machines or the dryers and moved them," Wolfe suggested.

"But then why would he bother with the detergent?" Faith asked. "It's kind of a mess. Even if the books were wrapped up well."

"You're probably right," Wolfe said. "Perhaps Derek thought the machines were too obvious and easy to check. So which is he? Victim or thief?"

Faith turned toward the half-empty box and looked at the traces of detergent on the floor. "There's only one way to find out."

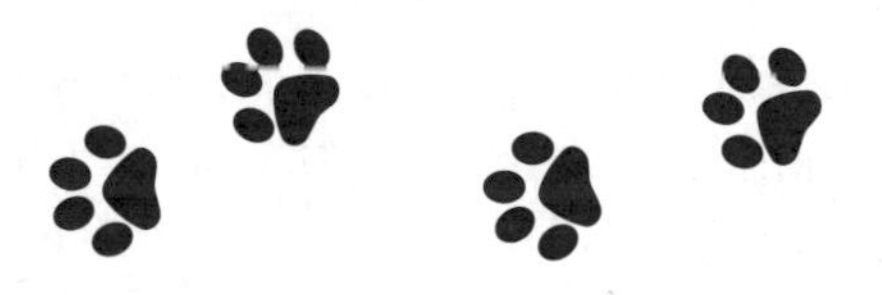

They found Derek, Skip, and Rob sitting at the card table in the billiard room with Petie asleep at Skip's feet. For once the three men weren't playing poker.

"I think we should do it." Rob sat hunched over the table, his mouth in a tight line. "We've all searched separately, but I think it's time we organize. No more of this amateur stuff. If we lay out a grid and—" He broke off, noticing Faith and Wolfe.

"May we join you for a moment?" Faith asked.

She sat in the chair Rob pulled out for her, and Wolfe sat opposite her, between the other two Drelincourts.

Derek gave Faith his usual feral smile. "Officer Drelincourt was just telling us how to find the missing books. I wouldn't mind helping, of course. For Uncle Max's sake, I think the collection ought to stay together." Impossibly, his grin turned even more smug than before. "Not that I'm worried for myself."

"I'm not sure if you should be worried or not," she told him. "A little while ago my cat brought me a pull strip off a box. A detergent box."

"I guess cats will play with anything. What's that got to do with us?"

"We figured out it was from one of those large detergent boxes in the manor laundry room," Wolfe said. "The industrial strength kind, my mother calls them. Really big. Lots and lots of room."

Derek shrugged, no less smug than before.

"It's only about half-full now," Faith said.

Derek's eyes widened. "What?"

"Whatever somebody hid in there is gone now."

Derek gaped at her for a moment and then tore out of the room.

Petie woke suddenly and barked at him, but Skip quieted him with a sharp command.

"What's going on?" Rob asked. "Where'd he go?"

"Down to the laundry, I expect," Wolfe said. "The box of detergent that was new and should have been full is about half-empty now. We decided Derek had hidden his books there—although how he thought a member of the housekeeping staff wouldn't find them, I don't know. They're not there now. We assumed he had moved them again or someone else had taken them. I guess now we know."

"Did he tell either of you where he hid his books?" Faith asked.

Rob and Skip both shook their heads.

"He isn't exactly the trusting type," Rob said.

Skip snorted. "I guess he won't be crowing anymore about how he's too smart to let somebody take his books."

"Where was he off to?" Morris peered into the billiard room as if he were making sure the way was clear. "He nearly ran Gord and me down."

Next to him, West nodded.

Rob looked at both of them, his face stern. "Where have you two been lately?"

Morris shrugged. "Trying to stay out from underfoot, right, Gordo? Ms. Russell, she likes it best that way."

"Have either of you been in the laundry room?" Wolfe asked.

"Laundry room?" Morris glanced at West. "You didn't need something outta there you didn't tell me about, did you?"

West shook his head.

"Gord says no."

Before anyone could question them further, Derek stormed back into the billiard room, dark eyes blazing. "I want to know who's behind this, and I want my property back. Now."

"We're working on it," Wolfe said.

Derek thrust out his chin. "And exactly how have you been working on it?" He eyed Morris and West. "Evidently anyone and everyone has access to the whole place."

Wolfe's mild expression didn't change. "We've been doing some investigating. Searching in the—"

"I tell you where we ought to be searching," Derek interrupted. "On the third floor where you live. Has anybody searched up there?"

Skip and Rob stared at Derek.

"Hold on," Rob began.

Wolfe held up one hand to stop him. "The books couldn't be up there. It's off-limits to the guests and most of the staff."

"You could have taken them up there yourself." Derek clenched his fists, and his face was spotted with red. "They could be sitting on a shelf in your living room for all any of us know."

"And why would I do that?" Wolfe's voice and expression were coldly controlled.

"Those books are valuable," Derek spat. "You know that as well as anyone. And you wanted them. Why wouldn't you take them if you thought you could?"

"Don't be ridiculous. After everything that's happened, I could never sell them without it being obvious that I was the one who stole them. I couldn't even display them in the manor library. I was willing to buy them, and I wasn't trying to undercut the price either. You can do the research yourself. Faith put together a good bid, fair to you and to me."

"Free's better than fair, isn't it?" Derek's belligerent expression didn't change. "How do we know you're not one of those people who just wants a collection, whatever it is, and doesn't mind keeping it in a basement or an attic as long as he knows he's got it all for himself? How do we know what you've been up to all this time?"

"Come on, man." Skip put one hand on Derek's arm. "Sit down and—"

"No." Derek jerked his arm away. "It makes perfect sense. Nobody's allowed up there. He owns the place, right? Who else would have keys to everything and a whole staff of people to cover for him? I don't know why I didn't think of it before."

Rob shoved a chair toward Derek. "Sit down and shut up for a minute. You're talking crazy."

Derek flung himself into the chair, glaring at Wolfe.

Wolfe seemed unimpressed. "I know things are tense right now, but even if I were the biggest con and thief in the world, it would be idiotic for me to try to steal those books from you and your family. They're valuable but not more valuable than my reputation and the income I get from Castleton Manor. Forget about right and wrong and whether or not I know the difference, but I'd be a pretty sorry businessman to risk a large part of my livelihood for something like this, especially when I can offer a fair price for the collection."

Derek glared at him for a few seconds more and then blew out his breath. "Okay, fine. Maybe you're right. But there has to be something we can do. This whole thing doesn't even make sense."

"Come on," Rob said, standing and pulling Derek up with him. "Why don't you and me and Skipper play a little pool and take it easy for a while? We can get back to work on the investigation after lunch. Those books aren't going anywhere in this weather."

Derek stood stiffly for a moment, and his habitual smug expression returned. "Why not?" Again he eyed the two men from Vegas, then gave Skip a sardonic smile. "You can even bring your pals along."

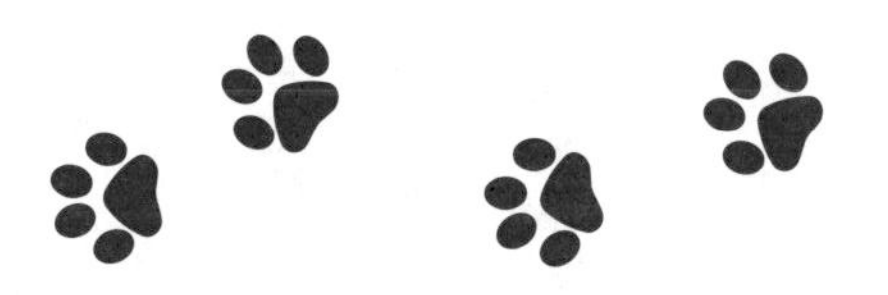

While the Drelincourts played billiards, Faith and Wolfe gathered Brooke, Midge, and Eileen for an impromptu meeting down in the kitchen.

"Derek's books are gone," Faith announced.

Wolfe nodded as the other three women exchanged startled looks.

"Are they all gone now?" Midge asked. "That's an awful lot of books."

"As far as we know, Michelle is the only one who still has hers, and she keeps them with her in that carry-on bag. Locked, of course."

"So what now?" Brooke glanced toward the closed door that led to the corridor and the stairs up to the butler's pantry. "The weather's likely to break pretty soon. And while that would be great news for everyone who'd like to have contact with the rest of the world, it means whoever has those books might be able to smuggle them out."

Faith smiled. "Not if we find them first."

19

"What are we going to do?" Eileen asked, her eyes sparkling.

Faith couldn't help smiling wider at her aunt's enthusiasm. "*We* are going to make our thief tip his hand."

"How?" Midge asked, leaning forward eagerly. "Do you know who it is?"

"I have my suspicions," Faith said. "All this time we've been snowed in like they were in *Murder on the Orient Express*, and I've been wondering if, as in the book, there was more than one person in on the crime, providing mutual alibis, planting evidence, that sort of thing. But now I'm wondering if it isn't more like *And Then There Were None*."

"Except for the murders," Wolfe put in.

Midge nodded. "Thank goodness for that."

"We're trapped here like the people on that island," Faith said, "and one after another, no matter how closely we watch, our unseen villain commits another crime. We just have to stop the thief before the last of the books disappear."

"And find the others," Wolfe added.

"How are we going to do that before the ice melts?" Brooke asked.

Faith leaned closer. "We call in an expert."

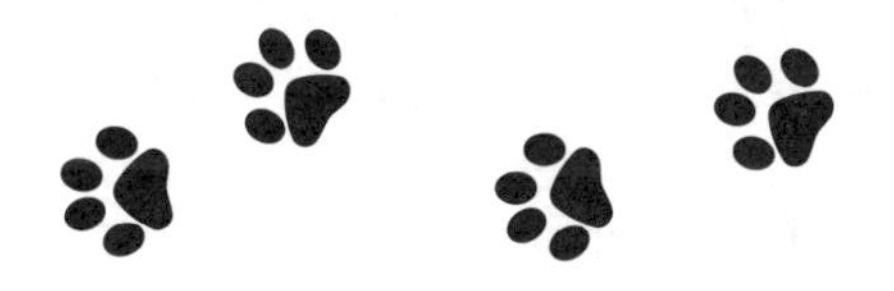

It was quiet at the dinner table that night. Except for

Ahnold, who had been left in his room napping, all the pets were lounging quietly beside their owners. There was talk of the weather. There was always talk of the weather. Everyone was worn-out with talking about the weather, but at last there was the possibility that their enforced confinement would soon be over. It looked like the storm had ended, and it was starting to warm up.

There was the usual discussion of the missing books, the usual wary glances, slightly veiled accusations, and bewildered sighs. Faith, Brooke, Eileen, Midge, Wolfe, and Marlene had fallen into the habit of eating every meal with the Drelincourts. The Mob Guys, as Eileen liked to call them, still ate in their own rooms. Faith wondered if that was helpful or harmful. Didn't that give them the perfect opportunity to prowl around on the second floor while everyone else ate? Still, she and her friends would find the thief soon enough. She was sure of it.

"We have to do something right away," Faith told everyone. "The storm is over, and you'll be leaving soon. Whoever has the books will be able to get them out of the manor."

"But the thief won't have the whole collection." Michelle patted her carry-on. "I'm not letting go of mine."

"I can't wait to get out of here," Skip said, glumly taking a bite of the black-bean soup Brooke had made to start off the meal. "I sure needed the money from those books, though."

"Who cares about them?" Tilly said. "I'm sick of the whole thing. Let's just enjoy being together, right, Uncle Max?"

Mr. Drelincourt smiled. "That was all I wanted in the first place. The books . . ." He sighed. "Well, I was hoping they'd stay together, but maybe they'll be found."

"I still think it's a shame to sell them off," Lloyd said, dabbing his mouth with his napkin. "They should stay in the family."

"They were never going to stay in the family," Mr. Drelincourt reminded him. "But if they'd been sold to the manor, at least they'd be together."

The Drelincourts started to bicker again over whether or not the books should be sold when Laura came in and said something quietly to Marlene.

Marlene nodded and then cleared her throat. "Excuse me, everyone. Everyone."

The multiple conversations abruptly stopped.

"Thank you," Marlene said. "I'm sorry to interrupt, but I've been told that power is about to be restored to the manor, so we'll be switching off the generator. I understand there may be a brief period when we won't have electricity, but it shouldn't last for more than a minute or two. Enjoy your meal."

Dinner was pleasant and—apart from Tilly losing an earring and getting Lloyd to help her crawl around under the table to find it—uneventful. Afterward, since it seemed there was little time left to find the missing books, everyone headed upstairs to conduct a search using Rob's grid system.

They had just made it to the hallway when everything went black.

Alice gasped.

Tilly's soothing voice came from the center of the room. "It's all right. They said it would be for only a minute."

In the darkness, there was the sound of a door opening and closing and then more footsteps.

"What's the hubbub?" Morris said. "I thought there was a generator."

"We're switching back to regular electricity," Wolfe said calmly. "I'm sure it'll be over soon."

There was a brief period of low chatter that grew more and more agitated when the lights did not come back on.

"That's a long minute or two," John said. "Ahnold's going to be wondering what's happening."

"The big lummox is probably still asleep," Derek told him.

"Anybody got a lighter?" Rob asked, eliciting a chorus of negative responses and the rustle of hands in pockets.

Everyone was milling around now, grumbling about the darkness.

"Watson will be having a heyday running around in the dark," Faith said. She was wondering if her voice wasn't a shade too loud when the lights snapped back on.

"That's more like it." Skip blinked, and then a huge smile crossed his face. "Hey, Petie, maybe the Internet will work, and we can check up on our leagues. What do you think?"

The dog yipped at him and wagged his tail.

"Let's get back to the search," Rob said. "Derek, you and Skip—"

"Nobody move," Michelle said.

Everyone turned to her.

Her carry-on was gone.

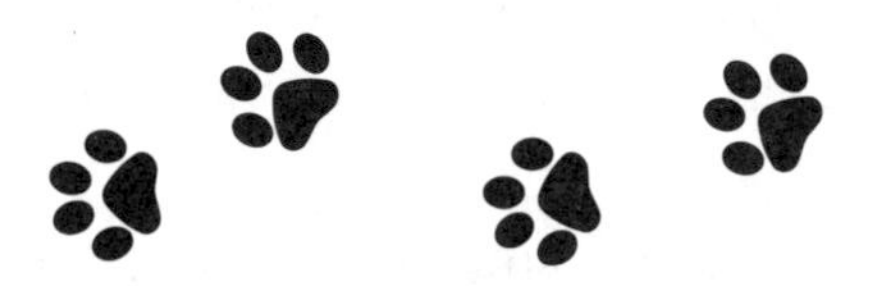

"Did I do all right?" Laura asked once the search was over and the Mob Guys and the Drelincourts had returned to their rooms.

"Perfect," Faith said. "We couldn't have done it without you."

As Faith had expected, there was no sign of any books in the Christie collection and no sign of Michelle's carry-on. It wasn't a large bag. It could have been hidden almost anywhere. And that was what she'd been counting on.

"So what do we do?" Eileen asked.

"We wait until morning," Faith replied.

"What?" Brooke said. "Why? Why not go ahead now? What if the thief figures out what we're doing?"

"We have to wait," Wolfe said. "It won't do any good to try it now."

Faith nodded. "He's right. Don't worry. Our thief was quick to snap up the bait, and now it's up to us to do the reeling in. All of you get a good night's sleep. Tomorrow's a big day."

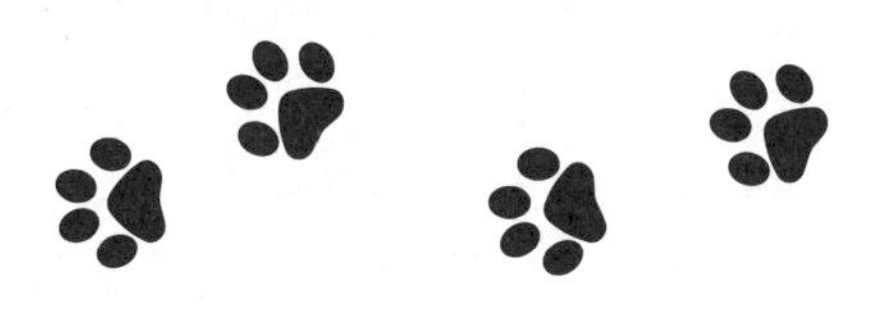

The next morning everyone gathered around the table in the breakfast room.

"What are they doing here?" Skip asked, his voice low as he glanced over at Morris and West seated at the end of the table.

"I believe Mr. Jaxon invited them," Faith said, trying her best to keep her excitement from showing on her face. "He has some good news for everyone."

Wolfe toasted the table with his cup of coffee. "I think you'll all be pleased to know that outside this morning it's a balmy thirty-four degrees. We've got the staff clearing the road."

"They are," John said. "I saw from my window. What a relief. Ahnold and I will be glad to go home."

"But what about the books?" Nadine demanded, her arms crossed over her chest. "Where are they? How will we get them back?"

"We ought to have something we can take back to our boss," Morris said pleasantly. "It would be imprudent for us to show up in Vegas empty-handed."

Skip leaned down to pet his dog, saying nothing.

"Don't worry," Faith told everyone. "Since we haven't been able to find the books, I've arranged for the services of an expert tracker. Ahnold."

"Don't be ridiculous," Derek protested. "He does fine with his stuffed animals, but there's no way he could track our books."

Wolfe stood, leaving his coffee and breakfast unfinished. "I suppose we're about to find that out. Will you all please follow me?" He led the group up the stairs and then stopped. "John?"

John made a little clicking noise with his tongue, and Ahnold got to his feet. "All right, Ahnold. Find it. Go on. Find it!"

The German shepherd sniffed the air and began looking around.

"Maybe we're searching on the wrong floor," Wolfe whispered to Faith.

"If we are, then we can take him downstairs," she whispered back. "But our thief mostly got the books from up here. This is where the carry-on disappeared, and this is where all our visitors' rooms are. It's the most likely place."

The dog wandered along the corridor, head up and sniffing, and finally made a beeline to one of the closed doors.

The door to Alice's room.

Alice turned to John, bewildered. "What's he doing?"

Ahnold whined softly and pawed at the door.

Alice. Faith thought back over the incidents of the past few days. Was there any reason Alice couldn't have taken a passkey and gotten in and out of the rooms whenever she wanted? And she had been sitting next to Tilly at dinner the night Tilly was drugged. She had come to get Faith's help afterward, but there was no reason she couldn't have taken away Tilly's books before then.

Alice had said that her husband had plans for the money she would get from the sale of her books. Could she have wanted to bring home even more? Or did she just want to keep the collection safe from him and the others who wanted to sell? She seemed so sweet. Even now, Faith couldn't quite believe it of her.

"Maybe you'd better open it," Wolfe said, his face grave.

"What are you saying?" Tilly placed herself between him and Alice. "She hasn't done anything. You have no right—"

"I don't mind," Alice said and unlocked the door. "Just be careful. Lucy—"

The dog forced his nose and then his head and shoulders into the opening of the door and loped into the room.

Faith and several of the others followed him inside.

At once, Ahnold crouched down and wriggled under the bed.

With a hiss, Lucy bolted out and dashed into the bathroom and hid behind the shower curtain.

"Find it!" John urged.

Ahnold was still nosing around under the bed. The dog backed out into the room again with a little stuffed pig in his mouth.

"How'd that get in here?" Alice asked. "I don't understand."

"I'm sure it was Watson," Faith admitted. "I saw him with it the other day and meant to get it back, but it slipped my mind. I'm sure he was just trying to impress Lucy."

Ahnold looked expectantly at John.

"Good boy." John accepted the toy and rewarded him with a treat and a pat. "Good boy."

Derek and Rob were both searching the room, opening drawers and the closet door.

Rob even poked under the bed, but there was nothing there now. "Clean as a whistle," he said. "Sorry, Alice honey."

"I told you I don't have the books. I don't know where they are. And what does the dog's toy have to do with the books anyway?"

Faith mentally crossed her fingers for the lie she was about to tell. "We were hoping Ahnold would be able to track John's scent on his share of the Christie books."

Mr. Drelincourt sighed. "It's all right, Alice. They had to look. It was sort of a long shot anyway. Well, now what do we do? Go back downstairs and talk it over?"

"Can he keep going?" Faith asked John.

John patted his dog's head. "Sure he can. Come on, Ahnold. Find it."

Immediately the German shepherd nudged John's hand that held the pig.

"No, Ahnold," John said. "Where's the moo-moo? Find it. Find the moo-moo."

"Moo-moo?" Tilly demanded. "What does that even mean? I thought he was tracking John's books."

The dog raised his head, sniffing again, and wandered out into the corridor. He looked from side to side, still sniffing, then made his way toward the end of the hallway. Alice's room was closest to the stairs. The rest of the rooms occupied by her family were beyond hers.

Ahnold trotted past Derek's room. Then past Eric's, Rob's, and Lloyd's. He paused in front of Skip's door, sniffing before moving along much more slowly, his liquid dark eyes full of intelligence. Finally he stopped, and his breathing came a little faster as he pawed the door.

The door of the Agatha Christie Suite.

Mr. Drelincourt frowned. "What is he after this time?"

"Really now," Lloyd said, his face reddening. "You're not saying Uncle Max has anything to do with the missing books, are you?"

"That's more ridiculous than accusing Alice." Tilly crossed her arms. "John, you ought to stop."

John looked at her and then at his uncle and then at the dog still pawing the door. "I don't know, Til."

Mr. Drelincourt frowned again. Whether it was at his nephew or not, Faith couldn't quite tell. Or was he trying to figure out what to do next?

Mr. Drelincourt straightened his shoulders. "Go ahead." He unlocked the door and pushed it all the way open.

Ahnold padded inside, sniffing the room, going to the foot of the bed and then to the closet door and then back to the bed.

"Find it," John urged.

Ahnold sniffed the air again, walked out of the room, and came back inside.

Rob looked at his uncle uncertainly. "You won't mind if we have a little poke around, will you? Somebody could have hidden the books in here to frame you."

Derek was already examining the space under the bed.

Mr. Drelincourt's mouth was taut. "Do what you need to do."

"Uncle Max," Tilly protested, "you don't have to let them."

Ahnold pawed at the closet door, whining.

"If there's something to be found," Mr. Drelincourt said, "then it needs to be found now."

He opened the closet door himself, and Ahnold bounded inside.

Faith could see nothing in there but hanging clothes, shoes lined up neatly on the floor under them, and presumably empty suitcases on the shelf above. Or *were* they empty?

Ahnold was mostly hidden by the clothes, but he stood on his hind legs, front paws braced against the wall, head up, barking.

"Is there something in those suitcases?" Nadine asked.

Tilly glared at her.

"There's no reason we shouldn't see, is there?" Nadine pulled the smaller bag down from the shelf and then the larger one. "It's okay, right, Uncle Max?" She put both bags on the bed.

But Ahnold didn't seem interested in them. He was still at the back of the closet, pawing and huffing and making little barking sounds.

"Ahnold," John said, "come on, boy. Over here."

The dog hesitated, his forehead wrinkled, and then he came obediently to the foot of the bed.

"Find it," John said. "Come on."

After Ahnold sniffed again, he returned to the closet, pawing at the back wall.

Derek pushed the hanging clothes to one side, and he and Rob inspected the wall.

"Nothing here," Derek said, scowling at the dog. "Stupid mutt."

Ahnold was too busy trying to dig through the wall to pay any attention to him.

"What's wrong with him?" Eric asked.

Skip tried to pull his own dog out of the way. "Cut it out, Petie. There's nothing there."

"That's not what Ahnold thinks," John said. "What's on the other side?"

"Just the closet next door. The Jane Austen Suite." Wolfe squeezed into the closet next to the German shepherd. "What do you think, boy? What's there?"

The dog gazed at him hopefully, panting and whining.

"The problem with this house," Wolfe said, kneeling down so he could examine the baseboard, "is that there are many nooks and crannies even I don't know about. That's what makes it so hard to do a thorough search of the place. It's quite possible that someone found a good hiding place"—he pressed a little groove toward the corner of the closet, and there was a metallic little *snick*—"we weren't aware of." He pressed the wall, and it swung back.

Ahnold immediately shoved his way inside and barreled into the stack of paper-wrapped objects concealed there.

There was a collective gasp of surprise.

"The books!" Michelle burst in and grabbed the package Ahnold was pawing at. "My books!"

"*Our* books," Eric corrected her, slipping Don Quixote into his pocket and then passing the other packages out to Rob's and Derek's waiting hands. "How'd he find them?"

Ahnold was at Michelle's feet, tail whipping back and forth as he fairly danced with eagerness.

She pulled off the paper, revealing *The Murder of Roger Ackroyd*, and opened the front cover. There was a small square of worn, stained brown corduroy inside.

Ahnold barked at it.

John knelt beside him and gave him a treat. "Good boy. Good, good boy."

"What is it?" Alice asked, baffled. "And why is it in there?"

Faith picked up the square of fabric. "We put it there. It used to be part of Ahnold's stuffed cow." She petted the dog's head. "Sorry, boy."

John grinned. "I told you Ahnold could find it no matter where it was."

"Now we know where the books are," Eric said, "but not who put them there."

"It seems fairly obvious to me." Faith raised an eyebrow at Mr. Drelincourt. "Who else could have gotten in and out of that closet so easily? It must have been disappointing when your father left the collection to your nieces and nephews and not to you. I can tell it means a lot to you. I suppose you didn't really want to see it sold off. Still, it wasn't very considerate of you to steal them from your own family."

The other Drelincourts appeared stunned.

Morris nudged West, his eyebrows raised as if to say, "Who knew?"

"Uncle Max," Tilly breathed, "tell them it's not true."

Mr. Drelincourt merely stood there, tight-lipped and stone-faced.

By then Rob and Derek had piled all the books on the bed. Nadine was opening various ones, confirming that they were the first editions they had lost.

"All the books are right here," Nadine said, her words spilling out rapidly as she pulled the wrapping off *Five Little Pigs*. "We can take them back, and it's all over, right?"

"That one's mine, thank you." Rob snatched the book from her. "And I don't know about just giving the books back. Besides the thefts, there has been the attempt to defraud Mr. Jaxon." His mouth was a grim line. "If he decides to press charges, Uncle Max could be in a lot of trouble. He might even face some jail time."

"Rob," Tilly protested, "you can't do that. You can't do that to Uncle Max."

"We wouldn't want to press charges against Uncle Max," Eric said. "We couldn't."

Several of the others echoed him.

"I wouldn't be the one doing anything," Rob said. "The law's the law. What was the plan, Uncle Max? Were you going to sue the manor because the books were stolen?"

"I only wanted to see you all together one final time," Mr. Drelincourt said, and there was a sadness in his expression, a weariness more profound than before. "There was no intent to defraud. The books have been found and can be returned. There's no need for criminal charges, is there? Surely—"

"What happens next will be up to the local police," Wolfe said, his eyes flinty. "Maybe they'll go easy on you since the books have been found. It's always hard to say when the law is involved."

"You can't do this," Tilly insisted.

"Hush now," Mr. Drelincourt said. "Don't say anything else. It will all be taken care of."

"I can't." Tears filled her dark eyes, and she dashed them away with one hand. "I can't just hush. It's not fair. It's not right." She met Wolfe's gaze, her chin raised defiantly. "You can't have Uncle Max arrested. He doesn't know anything about this. He didn't take the books. I did."

20

"I'm sorry, Tilly," Faith said, and she truly was. "I thought Ahnold would be able to find the books, but that still wouldn't tell us who took them in the first place. I didn't think the thief, whoever it was, would let your uncle take the blame."

Tilly looked ashamed and embarrassed. "I guess I'll have to go to jail then."

"No, of course not." Rob put his arm around Tilly's shoulders. "We got all the books back. Mr. Jaxon still wants to buy them, I think. Nobody's going to press any charges. I only said that so whoever was behind this would speak up."

"Really?" She drew a shaky breath.

"But we would like to know how you did it," Faith said. "This secret room sure came in handy. How did you find it? And how did you get in and out of here without your uncle knowing about it?"

"Let's all go downstairs," Tilly suggested. "If you want to hear my silly plan, Uncle Max should sit down."

"And us?" Morris asked, nudging his companion. "Seeing as we're not suspects anymore, I'd kinda like to know how it all was worked."

Wolfe gave a wry laugh. "Why not?"

They all trooped down to the banquet hall and sat around the big table. Brooke rustled up some coffee for everyone.

Tilly began her story. "Uncle Max and I came to the Agatha Christie retreat here two years ago. He had the Christie suite, just like now, and I had the same room next door. I accidentally discovered the entrance to the secret room in the back of my closet then and found it went through to Uncle Max's room. I didn't think much about it at the time.

"When Uncle Max said he wanted us all to get together, I told him this would be the perfect place. I knew Skip and several of my cousins wanted to sell the books, and I wanted to keep them, even if nobody knew I had them. I didn't want them sold off. As soon as we got here, I swiped one of the passkeys from the front desk when you were talking to my uncle." Tilly glanced at Marlene and winced slightly. "Sorry."

Marlene managed a semigracious nod and accepted the key Tilly offered.

"Anyway," Tilly continued, "I sneaked into their rooms the first night, Alice's and Skip's and Eric's, while everybody was downstairs. It wasn't hard then. Nobody suspected anything. John's was more difficult, with Ahnold there."

John frowned at her.

"I'm really sorry," Tilly told him. "I know I scared you, but I made sure ahead of time that the drug wouldn't hurt him. I wouldn't ever hurt him."

John's expression softened, and he ruffled the dog's thick fur. "Yeah, I know. It's okay."

Tilly drew a deep breath. "After that, I went into Nadine's room with the passkey while she was in the bathtub and took her books."

Nadine gave her a dirty look but said nothing.

"What about you?" Alice asked. "Weren't you afraid to take that much medication?"

Tilly shook her head. "I never took any."

"But Lloyd—," Derek protested.

"I was in on it with her," Lloyd interrupted. "Not at first, but when she told me why she wanted the books and asked for my help, I agreed. Tilly and I didn't think selling off the books would be the right thing to do. It was easy enough for me to take a peek and say she had been drugged. And then I gave her my own books later on and said they'd been taken. Sorry, everybody."

"And Rob's?" Michelle asked. "He had his with him. How'd you get them without him knowing about it?"

"Mind if I take a guess?" Faith asked. "Rob had his books in one of those laundry bags the manor uses. There are plenty of them in the storage room near your rooms. It wouldn't take much to fill them with books from the manor library and then switch them out when Rob wasn't paying attention. When you two were playing billiards maybe?"

Lloyd nodded. "I had the second bag waiting under the table, and when Rob was lining up his shot, I pushed his bag back and pulled the second one forward so he'd think it was his."

Tilly turned to Rob, a hint of a grin playing over her lips. "Some detective you are."

"Oh, an inside job, eh?" he said in a bad attempt to sound like a gangster in an old movie. "I'll get you for that, see?"

Tilly bit her lip, seeming to fight a giggle and tears at the same time. "Serves you right for scaring me about sending Uncle Max to jail."

"Yeah, I suppose. I guess that makes us even."

"Then I found where Derek had hidden his books in the detergent downstairs," Tilly said. "He didn't think anyone would figure it out since they weren't doing laundry until the power came back on."

Derek crossed his arms over his chest. "What gave me away?"

"You had bits of detergent in the stitching of one of your shoes. That was right after you started bragging about nobody finding your hiding place. I just put two and two together and found the books."

"Genius," Derek muttered.

"And that left Michelle's, and you all set it up well," Tilly said.

"We had to do something before you got away with the books," Faith said. "I didn't think you'd pass up the opportunity to get Michelle's carry-on while the lights were out."

"You were right," Tilly said. "While we were searching under the table for my earring at dinner—"

"Which you never actually lost," Lloyd said.

Tilly nodded. "I told Lloyd we had to get the last of the books when the lights went out."

"Where did you put the carry-on?" Faith asked.

"Actually, Lloyd got it first," Tilly admitted. "He passed it to me, and I slipped it into the housekeeping room that's right there where we were all standing. During the search, I made sure he and I covered that part of the floor. I came back in the middle of the night and moved the books into the secret room. I should have realized it was too easy and suspected it was a setup. It sure worked out great for you, with the generator going off just then."

Wolfe smiled. "That had nothing to do with the generator. One of the housekeepers flipped the switch when we were ready to let the carry-on be stolen and turned it back on a few minutes later."

"You remember Laura, don't you?" Faith asked. "Once I believed the bag was gone, I said the code word to turn the lights on: *Watson*."

"Michelle was pretty careless with her carry-on after keeping a death grip on it up to that point," Lloyd remarked. "Now I know why. She was in on it too."

"By the way, I'd like it returned. It's part of a set." Michelle eyed her cousin. "Innocent little Tilly, my foot."

"It's still in the housekeeping room," Tilly said. "I'll make sure it gets back to you. And I'll return what's left of the pills."

She took a steadying breath. "I'm sorry, everybody. I really am. But why didn't you have Ahnold track down the books last night? Why wait till this morning?"

"I told them to wait," John said. "I knew he could track the scent, even in a closed space, but it would be a while before the scent of that piece of fabric made its way out of Uncle Max's room and into the hallway. Without any air currents or anything, I knew searching last night would be a waste of time."

"I take back everything I said about the dog," Derek told him. "He's pretty smart after all."

"Still, that was a rotten thing to do, Til," Skip said. "Stealing from all of us."

"I know." Tilly hung her head. "It was awful. I just—I know Uncle Max loves those books, and there's nothing else to keep of his. He's pretty much sold off—"

"Tilly," Mr. Drelincourt said sharply with a warning shake of his head.

She looked at him defiantly. "He's pretty much sold off everything he's got, and it didn't even do any good."

Rob studied his uncle's face. "I knew there was something wrong. What is it? Why didn't you tell us?"

Mr. Drelincourt held up one hand. "I don't see a reason for any of you to go broke over this. Nothing can be done now, and there's no use throwing good money after bad."

"But what is it?" Rob asked.

"Pancreatic cancer," he said tightly. "It's all right. I've made my peace. I only wanted to see everyone together again and know you would all be fine."

"And I spoiled the reunion for everyone." Tilly looked as if she might cry. "I'm so sorry, Uncle Max. I just didn't want you to lose everything you loved."

"They're only books." Mr. Drelincourt put his arms around Tilly and held her close. "They're nothing compared to you kids. I considered buying them myself to keep them together, but I can't possibly do that now. It was everything I could do to arrange this reunion. But since I've been here, I know I want the collection kept together, especially in such a beautiful place where they'll be cared for and appreciated."

"We'll certainly do that," Wolfe said softly, and then he smiled at Tilly. "Now that we have all the books, maybe tomorrow we can get back to business. Castleton Manor would be proud to be the permanent home of the Maxwell Drelincourt Collection. And you can all come back and see the books anytime."

Tilly wiped her eyes with the back of her hand and managed a bit of a smile of her own. "Thank you. I think that would be wonderful."

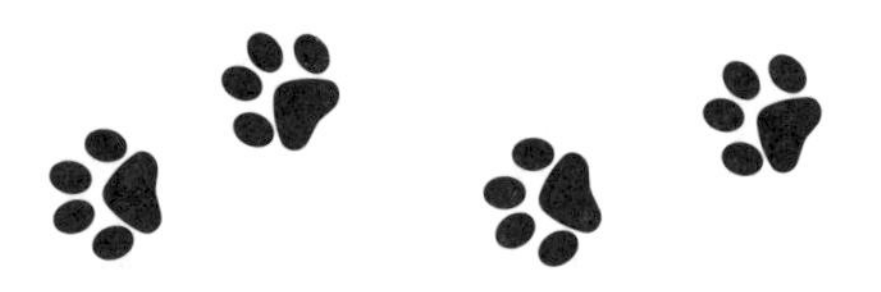

The next morning, after Faith and Wolfe had met with the Drelincourts and completed the purchase of the Agatha Christie collection, the ice had melted enough for her to take Watson back to the cottage.

"It's been quite an adventure for us," she told Marlene, "but I think we're both eager to return to normal. Is everything still all right with the Drelincourts? It was nice to see them hugging their uncle and actually paying attention to him."

"They seem to be getting along for a change," Marlene said. "I can't see it lasting long, but for now Mr. Drelincourt appears happy."

"Poor man. It must be hard to know you don't have much time left."

"At least he knows he's loved." Marlene's voice was cool and businesslike.

Faith didn't dare assume there was anything behind Marlene's words. Before she could think of anything else to say, Brooke, Midge, and Eileen came down to the front desk.

"It's been entertaining," Eileen said, "but it's time I went home."

Before Faith could reply, Morris and West entered the lobby.

"Ladies," Morris said, and then he gave Marlene a sardonic smile. "We've been informed that the tow truck has managed to get our car back on the road. Thank you, ma'am, for your hospitality in our time of need. It would have been imprudent for us to have kept driving in that weather."

Marlene nodded. "If you'll all excuse me, I have business to see to," she said briskly before walking away.

"Are you feeling better today?" Faith asked West.

He flushed slightly. "That doctor gave me some over-the-counter stuff that seems to help. Says he takes it himself."

"That's good." She turned to Morris. "What will your boss say when you get back to Las Vegas?"

"Mr. Jaxon paid Mr. Hamilton, and he signed the check over to Mr. Henderson." He patted his coat pocket, which rattled slightly in response. "It's a start." He made a slight bow, and then he and his confederate were gone.

"Hamilton?" Brooke asked, frowning. "I thought they were all Drelincourts."

Faith shook her head. "Skip and Tilly are Hamiltons, though their mother's maiden name was Drelincourt. Anyway, I hope Skip doesn't get himself into trouble with any other Mr. Hendersons after this."

Eileen chuckled. "Don't bet on it."

"I'll be so glad to get home to Peter and Atticus," Midge said.

"I know they missed you," Faith told her. "Just take it easy on the roads. I'm sure there's still plenty of ice and snow to watch out for." She shook one finger at Eileen. "You too."

"Don't worry," Eileen said. "I will. I'm excited about a fresh change of clothes."

"I won't argue with that." Brooke sighed. "Once I've cooked dinner for everyone, I'll be going home and giving Diva and Bling a big hug."

Eileen raised an eyebrow. "They're fish."

Brooke waved one hand. "Just figuratively. You know."

Faith laughed and hugged Eileen and Midge. "You two be careful. We should have a lot to talk about at the next meeting of the Candle House Book Club."

"I guess you and Watson will be headed home soon," Brooke said once Eileen and Midge were gone.

"If I can find him. I told him Lucy would be leaving with the rest of the Drelincourts, and I think he's set up camp outside her door."

"I found him." Laura carefully made her way over to them as Watson squirmed in her arms. "He was in the laundry room again. I think he was hoping to find another pull strip."

Faith took him and leaned him against her shoulder. "What did you do with the one you already had? No, don't answer that. I probably don't want to know."

Laura giggled. "I'm sure it'll turn up. Oh, did I tell you my big news?"

"What?" Brooke asked.

"Well, I've been thinking about this a long time, and thanks to Faith's encouragement, I'm going to go back to school when the summer session starts."

"That's great!" Faith hugged her, making Watson grumble

at the disturbance. "But I didn't do anything. In fact, I still owe you an apology for thinking you might have been involved in the situation with the books."

"No, it's all right. Really. You had to be sure. But you made me realize that I do want to be a librarian someday, and I won't ever do it if I don't take the first step."

"I'm so happy for you."

"Me too," Brooke said. "I don't think you can ever learn too much."

"But that's not even the best part," Laura said, fairly beaming. "Mr. Jaxon told me that if I show him my grades each semester, he'll pay for every class I get an A in. I can hardly believe it."

"That's fabulous," Faith told her.

"Yeah," Brooke said. "He's a great boss and a great guy."

"Oops." Laura glanced around guiltily. "I'd better get back to work or he won't be my boss much longer. See you later, Watson." With a wave, she hurried off.

Faith didn't envy her the week's worth of washing she was trying to catch up on, but at least some of the rest of the staff ought to be able to make it in to work today or tomorrow so she and the skeleton crew that had made it through the storm could get back to their regular jobs.

She was about to say as much to Brooke when she saw Rob coming down the stairs, headed straight for her.

"Hey, Faith, I was hoping to find you here."

"I need to get going," Brooke said with a knowing little smirk.

"Brooke—"

"Dinner won't cook itself. You and Watson be careful on that ice."

Watson scowled at her as she disappeared into the breakfast room.

"I hope I'm not interrupting anything," Rob said when he reached her.

"No, not at all." For some reason, Faith suddenly felt shy.

Maybe it was because she knew he would soon be gone. "I guess you'll be getting back to your boys tomorrow."

He smiled. "Yeah. Don't tell them, but I've missed the little guys." For a moment he hesitated. "I'm sorry we didn't have a chance to get better acquainted."

A tiny pang of regret surprised her, but then it was gone. "I'm glad you were here to help figure things out. It was kind of fun after all, wasn't it?" She held out her hand.

Rob clasped her hand in both of his, his gray eyes warm. "Now that I think about it, it really was."

Watson meowed and squirmed to get down.

Rob ruffled the fur on top of his head. "Okay, okay, we've all got to get home. You just remember what a lucky boy you are." He gave Faith one more smile, then went into the billiard room where his family was gathered.

She'd have to tell the family goodbye when they left tomorrow. For tonight, it would definitely be good to get home.

As Faith was getting ready to walk to the cottage, she was stopped by a familiar low voice behind her.

"It's been quite a week," Wolfe said. "I'm relieved everything turned out all right."

"Me too."

He glanced toward the billiard room door and the sound of talk and laughter. "It appears Mr. Drelincourt got his wish after all. The family seems a little closer now." His expression turned thoughtful. "I suppose you'll be sorry to see them go."

"Some of them. But things here were pretty nice before they came." Faith smiled into his eyes. "I can't complain."

Wolfe's mouth turned up on one side. "Great job, by the way. Those books are a wonderful addition to our collection. Thanks for everything you did to make it happen."

"It's my job," she said, gazing down at Watson as she stroked his ear, "but I *am* glad we could get the Christies for the library. It's an amazing set." She looked at Wolfe. "Oh, and thank you."

"Me?"

"Laura told me what you're going to do for her."

"Oh. Well." He shrugged. "I thought it was the least I could do after everything that happened. And I'm always glad to help people who are trying to better themselves."

"It was nice of you anyway." She settled her burden of squirming cat more securely against her shoulder. "I should get Watson back home before I officially start adding the Maxwell Drelincourt Collection to the library."

"May I see you to your door?"

Faith let him help her into her coat and then accepted the arm he offered. Brooke was right. Wolfe was a great boss and a great guy. And in spite of—or maybe because of—the mysteries and adventures she'd experienced since she came to Castleton Manor, Lighthouse Bay was a pretty great place to be.

Up to this point, we've been doing all the writing. Now it's *your* turn!

Tell us what you think about this book, the characters, the bad guy, or anything else you'd like to share with us about this series. We can't wait to hear from *you*!

Log on to give us your feedback at:

https://www.surveymonkey.com/r/CastletonLibrary

Annie's® FICTION